THE SUBSTITUTE CREATURE

77-98

Illustrated by Alashia Mitchell

Look for More SPINETINGLER Books by
M. T. Coffin
Coming Soon from Avon Camelot

BILLY BAKER'S DOG WON'T STAY BURIED
MY TEACHER'S A BUG

SPINETINGLERS

THE SUBSTITUTE CREATURE

M. T. COFFIN

AN AVON CAMELOT BOOK

THE SUBSTITUTE CREATURE is an original publication of Avon Books. This work has never before appeared in book form.

AVON BOOKS
A division of
The Hearst Corporation
1350 Avenue of the Americas
New York, New York 10019

Copyright © 1995 by Kathleen Duey
Excerpt from *Billy Baker's Dog Won't Stay Buried* copyright © 1995 by George Edward Stanley
Published by arrangement with the author
Library of Congress Catalog Card Number: 94-96265
ISBN: 0-380-77829-7
RL: 4.9

First Avon Camelot Printing: March 1995

CAMELOT TRADEMARK REG. U.S. PAT. OFF. AND IN OTHER COUNTRIES, MARCA REGISTRADA. HECHO EN U.S.A.

Printed in the U.S.A.

OPM   10   9   8   7   6   5   4

I

Jace Morgan stood facing the doorway of room 37. He hated to go in before the bell rang, but he knew he should. Mrs. Dement was strict about tardies. If you weren't in your seat—*bam!* Detention. Jace sighed, watching the hallway crowds thin out.

"Hey!"

Jace turned. Molly Grover was rushing toward him. She was grinning. "Guess who we have today? Just guess." She spun in a circle, her reddish hair fanning out. "We have the new substitute."

Jace shrugged. "So what?"

Molly raised her shoulders, imitating him. "So he's really strange, that's what." Jace shook his head, but Molly was leaning toward him, her eyes wide. "Hailey saw him at lunch one day, sitting in his car. He was eating something . . ."

1

Molly whispered the last word and Jace couldn't hear her over the noise in the hall. Her eyes narrowed and she shook her head.

Jace pushed himself away from the wall, trying not to laugh. Molly loved rumors. He reached out and patted her shoulder. "We better get going."

"You'll see," Molly said, gesturing toward the classroom door.

Jace turned away to hide his smile. He slid into his desk just as the bell rang. The man at the front of the room stood up and nodded. "Good morning," he said slowly. "My name is Mr. Hiss."

Jace stared as Mr. Hiss started talking. He was an odd-looking man, with eyes that seemed to bulge a little. A murmur of voices rose as he explained that Mrs. Dement was in the hospital. Mr. Hiss raised his hand to quiet the class. "Mrs. Dement is going to be fine. It isn't serious. And she asked me to tell all of you that she will miss you."

Jace watched Mr. Hiss's face as he spoke. He was weird-looking. That was probably why kids talked about him. His hair was black and shiny; his eyes were buggy and intense. He spoke carefully, pronouncing each word perfectly. Too perfectly.

"So I will be your teacher until Thanksgiving

vacation," Mr. Hiss told them, "or perhaps a little longer."

A murmur started at the front of the room and worked its way back toward Jace. He shifted uncomfortably in his desk chair. Everyone liked Mrs. Dement. Now she was going to be gone for almost two months.

Jace leaned forward, watching Mr. Hiss. When the substitute turned toward the blackboard, Jace tapped Abram Saeb's shoulder. Abram's glasses flashed in the classroom lights as he turned around. He grinned and Jace grinned back at him. They had been friends since first grade. "Maybe he'll be easier than Mrs. Dement," Abram whispered.

"Maybe," Jace whispered back. He glanced up. Mr. Hiss was busy going through a pile of papers on his desk. His slick black hair looked almost greasy. Mr. Hiss looked up and Jace quickly looked away. He didn't want to be caught staring.

"Now, you might be wondering what kind of teacher I am," Mr. Hiss said in a soft voice. He nodded, as if to answer himself. "You are probably thinking about whether I will be easier or harder on you than Mrs. Dement."

Abram made a little sound of astonishment and Jace shook his head. Had Mr. Hiss heard Abram's whisper? Jace glanced to his right and

3

found Molly looking straight at him. She nodded, like they were sharing a secret, then looked back at Mr. Hiss. Jace shivered, even though he felt silly. Mr. Hiss couldn't have heard Abram from the front of the room. The substitute did look creepy. And his voice was sort of weird, too, rough and papery.

"I'm a very patient person," Mr. Hiss was saying quietly. "I almost never get angry. But you have to do your work. I expect everyone to work, and to behave in a way that lets the rest of the class concentrate."

Then Mr. Hiss looked at the class. He was silent. The silence stretched out and filled the room. Mr. Hiss was quiet and motionless for so long that the kids all began to move around in their seats. Jace wanted to tap Abram's shoulder again, but he was afraid to. Was Mr. Hiss going to start class, or was he just going to stand there? Jace glanced at Molly again. She was looking at Mr. Hiss—everyone was.

Jace turned back. Mr. Hiss was still just standing there. He had kind of a dazed, dreamy expression on his face. After a few moments, Jace realized what Mr. Hiss was doing. He was looking at each student for a long time, then shifting his eyes to the next desk. Jace counted to a hundred inside his mind. Then he counted to a hun-

4

dred again. Slowly, methodically, like he was memorizing each face, Mr. Hiss made his way from one side of the class to the other. By the time he was halfway through, everyone was shifting around, rustling their papers and clearing their throats.

"Mr. Hiss is pretty strange," Abram said quietly, over his shoulder. Jace nodded and whispered an agreement. Then he caught his breath. Mr. Hiss was suddenly looking right into his eyes. Had Mr. Hiss heard Abram? Maybe he thought that Jace was the one who had said it. Jace glanced away. When he looked back, Mr. Hiss was still staring at him. He glanced away again, determined not to look back for a long time—so long that Mr. Hiss would have to look away. A second later he heard Abram suck in a quick breath and he realized it'd just been his turn—now Mr. Hiss had moved on. Abram fidgeted under the intensity of Mr. Hiss's gaze. Jace looked down at his own hands. The room was silent except for nervous noises. People shuffled paper and tapped pencils and scuffed their feet back and forth. "Does anyone here like to watch scary movies?" Mr. Hiss asked. His odd, precise voice crashed into the quiet room and Jace jumped. All over the room, people dropped pencils or papers, or just lurched in their desks, startled.

Jace saw Molly shaking her head. Mr. Hiss looked at her and she straightened up in her desk, blushing. Jace felt sorry for her. Mr. Hiss was giving her his bug-eyed stare now. She was getting a second turn. It wasn't fair. "Do you?" Mr. Hiss aimed the question straight at Molly.

"No," Molly said quietly. Her face was so pink she looked sunburned.

Mr. Hiss looked up. "Well?" He raised his eyebrows. It made his eyes look even weirder. "Doesn't anyone like the spooky stuff?"

Quite a few of the kids raised their hands. Jace didn't. He hated movies that scared him. He was brave in real life. Or at least, he was pretty brave. He had jumped into the canal pond once to save Jeremy Sping's little sister. But he had been afraid of the dark for a long time and he hated ghost stories. Jace frowned. Watching terrible things happen in a movie was definitely not his idea of a good time. Mr. Hiss was smiling at the boys who had raised their hands. A few more hands went up. Jace started to raise his, just to get on Mr. Hiss's good side. But then he didn't. It would be lying. Mr. Hiss nodded. "All right. Maybe we can talk about that later. Let's get going on today's work. The first thing I want to do is to assign an essay. I want you to write a paragraph about something you have always wanted to do." Mr. Hiss looked out over the class. "Anything you have dreamed about doing. I want you to think about it. Research if you need to. It'll be due tomorrow. Now, take out your reading books, please."

Jace risked a quick look at Molly. She didn't notice. She was still staring at Mr. Hiss. Jace glanced around the room. Everyone else was staring, too. And everyone looked uneasy.

After school Abram had to go to the library so Jace headed toward the busses alone. He was almost across the playground when he saw Molly. She grinned at him when he got close.

"See?"

Jace nodded reluctantly. "He's kind of odd."

Molly shook her head impatiently. "Kind of odd? If someone eats eyeballs for lunch, I'd say they're a little more than odd."

Jace almost stumbled. "He ate what?"

Molly nodded knowingly. "Eyeballs."

Abram suddenly ran past, shouting out a challenge to race. Automatically, Jace swung away from Molly and started running. But all the way home on the bus he thought about what Molly had said.

The next morning Jace got up and began dressing for school. He moved slowly, feeling lousy. He had done his homework. His essay was about learning to fly a plane. He thought it was pretty good. But he still didn't want to go to school.

"Are you all right?" his mother asked as she bustled from one side of the kitchen to the other. She gave him one of her sharp, X-ray looks. Then she answered herself. "You aren't all right. Something is worrying you." She slid a plate in front of him.

Jace shook his head. Usually he liked talking to his mother about things. But not this. This was too silly to admit. What would he say? My substitute teacher looks weird? He pronounces words too well? Molly Grover told me some stupid story even a second grader wouldn't fall for?

"Eat," his mother commanded. He looked up.

8

She was grinning. "Whatever it is, it will get better if you eat, and worse if you don't."

Jace shook his head again, but he smiled a little. His mother had made her voice creaky, and she suddenly had an accent. Her posture shifted and she was stooped, like an old peasant woman from some tiny European country. Jace smiled wider. His mother was an accountant, but she was also an actress. She had been in lots of plays, and she had even had a small part in a movie once. Usually, Jace forgot she was his mother when he watched her act. She seemed to change completely into the character she was playing; he knew that meant she was good. This morning she was having fun acting the part of an old peasant woman.

She leaned over the table, breathing heavily. "I mean it, Jace," she rasped. "If you don't eat for long enough, everything gets worse. Much worse." Her hands were trembly and she raked her hair back off her face. "Food. You can't know what it is to be without it, to survive what I have survived." Her voice was rough, pleading. "Eat, my son."

Jace laughed and started in on his eggs. His mother straightened and grinned, breaking character. She went back to the counter and rolled the top of his lunch bag closed. "If I'm gone when

9

you get home from school, call Abram's mother to tell her that you're here. I won't be later than four."

Jace nodded, then took a deep breath. "Mom?"

His mother turned around. "Mmmm?"

Jace looked down again and poked at his eggs. "We have a substitute."

"Has something happened to Mrs. Dement?" The concern in his mother's voice made Jace feel guilty. He was so worried about Mr. Hiss, he'd forgotten about Mrs. Dement going into the hospital. He wiped his mouth with his napkin and explained. "So everything is going to be all right," he finished. "She just can't teach for a while, until she gets better."

His mother smiled again, nodding. "So, how do you like the substitute?" Jace poked at his eggs again. He forced himself to eat a bite. Then he looked up. His mother was still looking at him. "He's all right, I guess."

His mother smiled wider. "Well. Give him a chance. Everyone likes Mrs. Dement, so it'll be hard for him. Substitute teachers have one of the hardest jobs in the world."

Jace nodded. He had never thought of it that way, but it was probably true. Everyone played tricks on substitutes. A few of the kids played really awful tricks. One substitute the year be-

10

fore had sat down on a tack. Jace squirmed in his chair, wincing. That would hurt. It would really hurt.

"Oh, my," his mother said. Jace looked up at her. She pointed at the clock. "Time to move it or miss it."

Jace wolfed down the rest of his breakfast then ran to his room to get his coat. It was still October but in the mornings it was starting to get pretty cold. He shrugged his jacket on, then slung his backpack over his shoulder. His mother handed him his lunch as he hurried down the hall. She kissed the air near his cheek and laughed. "I missed. See you this afternoon."

Jace nodded and headed out the door. Once he was outside, he pulled in a huge breath, then let it out and watched the steamy mist hang in the air. Jace began to feel good. The ground was hard with frost and the sidewalks were littered with fallen leaves. The air smelled good. Everything looked bright and clean. He started to trot along, ignoring the heavy bounce of his backpack.

"Jace!"

Abram's voice slowed him for a second, but he didn't stop. The bus was turning the corner. He pointed at it and Abram broke into a trot beside him. Mr. Gumplin had a rule. If he saw you coming, he would wait. But if you were more than a half-block away, he'd pretend he couldn't see you, especially if you were walking instead of running. Mr. Gumplin was a retired coach. He liked to see effort.

"We're going to make it." Abram panted out the words one at a time as he slowed a little to stay even with Jace. Jace nodded, but he kept up his pace. You could never be sure about Mr. Gumplin. Until you were close enough to actually make eye contact through the windshield, you couldn't relax. As he got closer, Mr. Gumplin revved the bus engine a little, but he braked, slowing. Finally, Mr. Gumplin looked at them. Jace slowed slightly. "He sees us."

He risked a grin at Mr. Gumplin as he and Abram stopped on the curb. Mr. Gumplin did not smile back, but he leaned forward as the bus squealed to a halt. The doors swung open. Jace and Abram thudded up the steps.

Jace let Abram sit by the window, then dropped into the seat beside him. The bus was steamy—way too warm. Abram pushed up his glasses. Jace wrinkled his nose. The bus smelled like wet wool. Everyone had worn a coat this morning. And it was noisy.

The gears chunked and Mr. Gumplin eased the bus forward. Jace watched the houses and lawns slide past the windows.

"I wish," Abram said suddenly, "that we didn't have a substitute."

Jace nodded. "Or at least not this one."

Abram looked over the top of his glasses at Jace and nodded. "I know what you mean. I don't like him."

Jace looked out the window again. "My mother said that subs have the hardest job in the world."

Abram made a sucking noise with his lips. "Oh, I don't know. I think that sewer workers have a worse deal. Or toxic waste handlers. Or people who get paid to test out new drugs or something."

"Okay, okay," Jace stopped him, laughing. "She just made me think about the fact that this isn't all that easy for Mr. Hiss, either. You know. Everyone likes Mrs. Dement. And now he has to take over with everyone being sort of unfriendly and everything."

Abram was nodding slowly. "I guess. But you still have to admit that he's a little weird."

Jace shook his head. "Maybe not. Maybe he just looks weird."

Abram laughed. "Good old Jace. Trying to be fair." He pushed his glasses up higher on his nose. "Maybe you're right."

Jace looked out at the trees. All the leaves were gone. It would snow before long. He glanced back at Abram. "Molly Grover told me something strange yesterday at recess."

Abram nodded. "Me, too. I think she told everybody."

Jace looked at him. "You believe it?"

Abram shrugged. "No. Of course not."

Jace nodded and turned to look back out the window.

When Mr. Gumplin opened the doors to let everyone out, Jace and Abram jumped up. They always tried to be the first ones off the bus. The bus got them to school nearly a half hour before the bell rang, and if they hurried, that was enough time to do something. Some mornings they played catch with Abram's baseball. Other mornings, when it was cold, they went into the library. Abram squinted up at the pale sun and shivered. "Library?"

Jace smiled at him. "Uh-huh." Then, without warning, he began to run. "Race you!"

"Cheater!" Abram accused, pounding along behind him. "If you win it's . . . because . . . you cheated."

Jace ran down the sidewalk, then cut into the grass when the crowds got too thick, zigzagging to miss a group of girls talking in front of the cafeteria. He was still ahead! It wasn't a fair race and he knew it. He also knew Abram wouldn't

14

quit or get angry. They had a pact. Whenever one of them wanted to race, the other had to at least try.

Jace swung around some boys playing soccer on the frozen grass. He risked a glance back. Abram had gained a little. The only way Jace could ever beat him was to catch him off guard. Abram was the fastest runner in the whole school.

"Cheater," Abram shouted from behind him as they leaned into the corner by the cafeteria. He looked back. Abram was catching up and they still had to cross the playground. Jace pushed his shoulders forward to keep his backpack from bouncing so hard. The grass was slippery with frost and he had to slow down to keep from losing his footing. But Abram had to slow a little, too, and when Jace glanced back, Abram was still a few strides behind. Jace took the shortest route across the playground, jumping the end of the slide and barely skirting the edge of the basketball court. He managed to stay just ahead of Abram. As they reached the library doors Jace threw his head back in triumph.

"I won!"

"Because you cheated." Abram was breathing hard and his face was flushed pink. His eyebrows were crunched together and he looked furious, but his mouth kept twitching. Jace knew he was about to start laughing. They had raced like this since first grade.

"I know you're faster," Jace admitted, looking as serious and sad as he could. "And so, I have to cheat."

Abram nodded slowly, pretending to address a group of kids who were walking by. "It's very sad. He runs like a turtle." Then Jace pretended to cry and Abram pretended to pat his back and comfort him.

"Are you two coming in?"

Jace jerked his head up, and Abram stepped back. It was Ms. Kosanovitch. She was tall and Jace had to look up to meet her eyes. "Yes," he managed. Ms. Kosanovitch was nice but she was also very strict.

"Well, then, come on," Ms. Kosanovitch said firmly and reached past them to swing open the door. Jace turned and went beneath her arm, with Abram right behind him. Once they were inside, Ms. Kosanovitch walked across the wooden floor to her desk where she slipped her coat off and began untying her scarf. Jace watched her for a second, then he looked out the windows. The rest of Cusick Elementary School was old, but the library was new. The windows were mirrored on the outside, so no one could see in. But from this side, they seemed tinted, turning everything a little darker and greener than it really was. Jace flinched when Abram poked him.

"Come on," he whispered. "Let's go before she starts keeping an eye on us."

Jace nodded. Ms. Kosanovitch was famous for giving kids her evil eye if they did things she didn't like.

They hurried to the study tables, and dropped their backpacks onto the floor. "You should look at the encyclopedias for that essay," Jace whispered. "The one that Mr. Hiss assigned yesterday. I wrote it last night. Or did you actually do your homework for once?"

Abram shook his head. "Of course not. What's yours about?"

Jace grinned. "Flying. Being a pilot." He shrugged. "I think it's pretty good."

Abram pushed his glasses up on his nose. "Maybe mine should be about skiing. I think it would be fun to ski. Or snowboard." His face lit up. "Snowboarding! Perfect subject."

"You aren't going to find snowboarding in the books here," Jace reminded him. "It's too new."

Abram took off his glasses and rubbed them on his shirt. "Probably not. I won't need to research, anyway."

"Will you boys stop whispering?" Ms. Kosanovitch was looking right at them. She didn't look

17

angry. But she didn't look away, either. Jace watched as her eyes narrowed and the small crease between her eyebrows got deeper. The evil eye was about to happen. Jace started off toward the encyclopedias. Maybe looking through reference books would take his mind off Mr. Hiss. It certainly would stop Ms. Kosanovitch's evil eye.

When Jace glanced back at the tables, Abram was leaning forward, writing furiously. Abram always let everything go until the last minute, but then he caught up. He could do homework faster than anyone Jace had ever known. And he usually got things right, too. He finished tests faster than anyone else. He had trouble with math, but he worked at it. His grades were good. Math was about the only subject that was hard for Abram. Jace shook his head and looked back at the bookshelves.

The reference section had three sets of encyclopedias. He stared at them for a few seconds, then reached out. It really didn't matter which volume he looked at. Abruptly, his attention was distracted by an odd choking sound. He looked up. No one was on this side of the library except for two girls who were looking at cat books. They were so quiet he hadn't even noticed them before. While he watched they stood up and headed for the exit door, gathering up their books and coats.

Jace started to reach for the encyclopedia once more, but the noise came again and his hand froze in midair. The muted choking sound got softer yet somehow more urgent. It sounded like someone was really strangling. But where? Jace stood up and quickly walked to the end of the shelves. He leaned to see up the next aisle. No one. And this was the last set of bookcases. He walked around to the back side of the shelves.

Along the wall there was only the drinking fountain, and a door. Jace stared at it. He had never really noticed it before. There was no sign on it, nothing to indicate where it led.

The sound came again. Someone was choking, gasping for air. In three quick steps Jace was standing in front of the door. The sound had come from behind it, he was sure. Jace hesitated for a second, then he grabbed the doorknob and pulled it open.

Jace just stood there, swaying back and forth on his feet. Mr. Hiss was inside the room, standing in front of a wall mirror. His back was toward Jace, and he apparently had heard nothing, because he didn't turn around. But Jace could see his face anyway, because of the mirror. Mr. Hiss's mouth was contorted into a grimace, and his hands and face were red and shiny. Red and shiny with what could only be blood.

Jace stood transfixed, unable to call out for help. Then, as he watched, Mr. Hiss suddenly grinned at himself in the mirror. It was a wide, weird grin. Startled, Jace stumbled backward, out into the library. The door slid out of his fingers and closed silently. He stood staring at it, too confused to do anything for a few seconds. Then, without thinking, he turned and almost ran back to the table where Abram was sitting, still working on his essay.

"Abram," Jace whispered fiercely.

Abram looked up and pushed his glasses higher on his nose. "What's wrong, Jace? Are you all right?"

Jace shook his head, then nodded, then shook his head again. "I just saw Mr. Hiss . . ." He glanced back toward the reference shelves which hid the door he had opened. "I saw him . . ." Jace turned back to stare into Abram's eyes. "I saw him . . ."

Abram shook his head. "What? You saw him . . . what?"

"He was . . . he was . . ." Jace rubbed his hand across his face. He took a deep breath, unable to finish.

Abram suddenly looked past him, his eyes widening behind his glasses. "Here he comes," Abram whispered. "Mr. Hiss is coming. Sit down." Jace whirled around, but Abram reached out and pulled him back down into the chair. "What's wrong with you, Jace?" Jace felt Abram's fingers digging into his shoulder. He wanted to explain. But he could only shake his head and turn back to stare at Mr. Hiss.

The substitute was walking across the library, smiling pleasantly, looking as normal as sunrise on Sunday. Jace swallowed hard. What had happened? Had Mr. Hiss just cut himself or something and then . . . ? Jace swallowed again. No. His face had been covered with blood. Covered. And his hands. And that weird grin . . .

"What's wrong?" Abram whispered again as Mr. Hiss passed their table. Jace tried to answer him, but his voice wouldn't work. He was shaking and he couldn't stop. Jace shook his head. How

21

could he explain what he couldn't understand himself? The bell rang.

Automatically, Jace stood up. "We had better get going," he managed.

Abram stood up, scooping his papers into a pile. "Yeah. Sure. But what happened? You looked so scared, or sick or something."

Jace nodded. He had stopped shaking at least. "I just thought I saw something." He cleared his throat. That had to be it. He had imagined the blood on Mr. Hiss's face and hands. There was no other explanation. Because of what Molly had said, he was imagining things. Jace avoided Abram's eyes. Abram was his best friend, but even Abram would think that this was stupid. Old scaredy-cat Jace, making up things. Jace, the one who hated scary movies and haunted houses and who had been afraid of the dark until he was eight. Jace took a deep breath. He was still a little afraid of the dark.

"Are you sure you're all right?" Abram was staring into his face. Jace managed to nod and Abram smiled. "We'd better hit it then, or we're going to be late." Abram crammed his homework into his notebook. Jace picked up his backpack. When Abram started for the doors, Jace was right behind him.

At first Jace's knees felt shaky. But as he

walked, he began to feel better. Everything around him was normal and bright. The kids were noisy and the air was cold and clear. Once they had crossed the playground and had started up the hill past the gym, Jace was pretty sure that the whole thing had been a trick of his imagination. Mr. Hiss couldn't have been that hurt, and then acted like nothing had happened a few minutes later. It wasn't possible.

Jace let out a big breath and smiled. He was glad that it hadn't been real. He might not like Mr. Hiss very much yet, but that didn't mean he would ever want him to be hurt. Jace clenched his hands into fists, then let his fingers curve loosely and relax. It was strange to think that he could have imagined something like that, but it was the only explanation. The light in the little room hadn't been that bright.

"Hey, Abram! Jace!"

Jace looked up. It was Brett Kirston, walking with Molly Grover. They were both laughing.

Jace nodded at them. "Hi."

Abram stopped and glanced at his watch. "We have about three minutes." Jace set down his backpack.

Brett said something in Molly's ear and they both laughed quietly. "Well, we still have the Substitute Creature," Molly announced as they

23

came up. "I wish Mrs. Dement hadn't gotten sick."

"Me, too," Brett agreed.

Jace watched Brett's face. He was smiling, like the whole thing was a big joke. He had been one of the first ones to raise his hand when Mr. Hiss had asked about scary movies. Brett was the last person Jace would ever tell about what he'd imagined in the library.

The warning bell rang and Jace picked up his backpack. "We'd better get going."

Brett poked Jace in his ribs. "You're always so worried about getting in trouble. Relax." Jace moved away, frowning. Brett was always making fun of someone.

Molly was shaking her head. "Brett . . ."

Jace looked at her. "It's okay, Molly."

Brett turned back and nodded. "Of course it is. Jace knows I'm just giving him a hard time. You guys see the new Plague of Hallowtown movie yet?"

Jace shook his head. Abram nodded. "Scary."

Brett laughed. "No, it wasn't. It was fake. You could tell that none of it was real. It wasn't scary at all. You might even have liked it Jace."

Jace nodded without looking at Brett. He wondered what Brett would say if he told him about what he had seen in the library. What you imag-

24

ined, Jace corrected himself, then he looked back at Brett. Brett acted so tough and so brave all the time. Maybe he was. But Jace sure got tired of hearing about it.

Molly started telling a long joke. It had a fish in it, and a couple of football players. Jace tried to listen, but he couldn't. It was getting late. He glanced up the hallway. The morning crowds were clearing out fast. Jace slung his backpack over his shoulder and started toward class. He heard Brett make a comment, but ignored him.

When he got to room 37, he glanced back. Abram was right behind him. They went through the door and down the second aisle between desks. Abram plopped into his seat with a sigh. Jace sat down behind him and took a deep breath before he allowed himself to look at Mr. Hiss. Then he felt silly.

Mr. Hiss was absorbed in reading something. He looked absolutely average. And he didn't even look up when the tardy bell rang. Kids were whispering, fooling around. Brett and Molly came through the door and hurried to their seats.

Abram turned to look at Jace, his eyebrows arched. He pushed his glasses up on his nose. "Good thing for those two that Mr. Hiss doesn't care about tardies."

Jace nodded. Mr. Hiss still hadn't looked up.

Jace glanced out the window, wishing that it was Saturday, and that he was at home. It was sunny. It'd be a great day for him and Abram to ride their bikes.

"Good morning," Mr. Hiss boomed out suddenly. Jace jumped in his seat, startled. He saw Abram twitch. There were nervous giggles all over the room. Jace glanced around, then back at Mr. Hiss. No one knew what to think. Jace could see Brett staring at the substitute teacher; his eyes were narrowed and angry-looking. Molly had her eyes down. Jace glanced around the room. Mr. Hiss had startled everyone.

"Let's begin, then," Mr. Hiss announced. "I like to start the day with math, while everyone has a clear mind. Please take out your math texts. And pass in the homework. All of it. Math papers and your essays, please." Jace took out his work and smoothed the paper. He tried to be neat, but it was hard for him. Cookie crumbs had crawled out of the corners of his backpack and somehow found their way onto his papers. There were only a few grease spots on today's math. That was better than usual, actually. Jace looked at Mr. Hiss, feeling a little self-conscious. Mrs. Dement was used to his papers. Mr. Hiss might say something.

When Jace tapped Abram on the shoulder to

pass the papers up, he whispered in his ear. "At recess let's get a basketball game going."

Abram nodded without turning around.

"All right," Mr. Hiss said loudly. "Open your books to page seventy-six. Let's look at the examples of fractions."

Jace tried to pay attention while Mr. Hiss was talking, but it was hard. Math came easily to him, and it was boring to have to sit and listen to everyone else's questions.

Abram's hand was in the air. Mr. Hiss pointed at him. "Yes?"

"So the bottom number is always the one that has to be the same?"

Mr. Hiss nodded. "Yes. Before you can work out the problem, you have to make sure that you are dealing with apples and apples."

Abram put his hand up again. "I don't understand."

Someone in the back of the room giggled. Jace knew without looking that it was Brett. Jace fought an impulse to turn around and glare at Brett. His mother said people like Brett were really insecure about themselves. Maybe that was true. Brett seemed to have to make a point of acting sure of himself all the time.

"I don't understand what apples have to do

with fractions," Abram said a little louder. Brett giggled again.

"Questions are never funny," Mr. Hiss said firmly.

Jace looked at him. His face was stern.

"I don't want anyone making fun of someone who is trying to learn."

Two or three kids turned around and Jace knew that they were looking at Brett. All the kids got tired of his teasing. They got tired of how tough he acted all the time, too.

"I won't hear any more of that, will I?" Mr. Hiss was looking over Jace's head, in just about the right direction to be staring at Brett. Jace hoped so. Brett had never listened to Mrs. Dement. Maybe he would listen to Mr. Hiss. That would be one good thing out of all this.

"What was your question again?" Mr. Hiss asked Abram. Abram stammered a little and Jace could see that the edges of his ears were red, but he managed to repeat the question.

Mr. Hiss explained, then went on with the lesson. Jace listened for awhile, then he began to look out the windows again. Daydreaming was a bad habit and he knew it, but he couldn't help it when he got bored. He doodled on his paper, trying to make himself pay closer attention, but Mr. Hiss was still explaining why the denominators had to be the same when you added fractions. Then he started explaining how you did it.

Jace yawned. It was sunny and beautiful outside. It almost looked like summer, except that the trees were bare, and Jace knew that it was cold. But still, it was easy to imagine that the brilliant sun was warm. Mr. Hiss's voice was soft and precise as he talked on and on. Jace watched him, trying to imagine his face all covered in blood, but he couldn't. It seemed incredibly distant and unreal. Maybe the light in the little room had been strange. Jace straightened up in his seat. Maybe there was a red bulb in the mirror light for some reason. Jace slid back down, sighing. Why would anyone put a red light bulb in a teacher's washroom? He shifted uncomfortably in his chair. There had to be some explanation.

Abruptly, Mr. Hiss turned from the blackboard and faced the class. "So for math, do the checkup problems on page thirty-four. Now, get out your reading books, please."

The room got noisy. Jace shoved his math book into his desk, then bent down and opened his backpack.

"Page forty-four," Mr. Hiss said over the commotion. "I want to hear you read aloud."

Jace heard a few of the kids groaning and he

felt sorry for them. In first and second grade he'd been afraid he'd never learn to read. It had seemed so easy for everyone else, and so hard for him. But now he liked it. He even liked reading aloud. Jace found the right page and looked at it.

"Brett, you start," Mr. Hiss said.

Brett began and the class quieted down. He read carefully, as though he were afraid to make a mistake. After a few pages, Mr. Hiss named someone else. When Jace's turn came, he tried to read smoothly.

After each student had read aloud, Mr. Hiss began talking about blended consonants. He began imitating cartoon characters saying words with the blended sounds. The class started laughing. Jace looked around the classroom. Everyone was interested, sitting up straight and having fun. Maybe things were going to be all right after all. Mr. Hiss was a pretty good teacher. It wasn't his fault that Mrs. Dement had gotten sick and it wasn't his fault his imagination had run away with him.

By lunch time, Jace had begun to feel almost normal again. After the long recess, he felt even better. He and Abram won their basketball game by a mile. After lunch, Mr. Hiss let them watch a film about the American Revolution. It was pretty interesting. Then, to finish up the day, Mr. Hiss talked about the film.

"Did you see the way they made it look like the cannon balls were actually landing and killing people?" Everyone nodded. Mr. Hiss smiled. "Of course you know that all of that is staged, that it isn't real." Everyone nodded again.

Mr. Hiss suddenly stood up and began pacing back and forth, talking. "The Tories were people who were still loyal to the English king. They were often persecuted by their neighbors. Revolutionaries sometimes stole their cows, or burned or stole their crops in the night. In the cities, Tory homes were burned down, and their children were chased and harassed."

As Mr. Hiss talked, Jace found himself imagining what it would have been like to be chased through the streets because of something his parents believed.

"What would it be like to live in a country about to go to war with a king?" Mr. Hiss mused. "It was a very confused time. No one knew what was about to happen. Think about it. You'd try to decide what was right, but also what was smart. No one wants to have his family hurt. No one wants her home burned. It took a lot of courage to be open about believing in either side."

Abram turned and whispered something out of the side of his mouth.

Jace leaned forward. "What?"

"Maybe he isn't so bad after all," Abram said a little louder. Jace nodded. Mr. Hiss was making history interesting.

". . . and so what I want you to do," Mr. Hiss was saying, "is to imagine being a Tory right before the Revolution began. I want you to write about an incident. You could write about going to the store, or about walking to see your father where he worked." Mr. Hiss looked at the ceiling, then back at the class. "Use what you know about the period and write something vivid. Make it as real as you can. What would happen? What would you be thinking about? What would you be scared of?"

Jace nodded, already thinking. This might actually be fun. If he were living back then, he might already be apprenticed to someone, learning a trade. What trade would he want? Maybe a silversmith, like Paul Revere. Or a printer like Benjamin Franklin. Jace was still thinking when the bell rang.

"The writing assignment is due next Friday," Mr. Hiss told them. "See you all tomorrow, then." Mr. Hiss sat down in his desk chair as they scrambled to pick up their books.

Jace zipped his backpack and stood up quickly. He and Abram started for the busses. But half-way there Jace stopped. "I forgot my math book."

Abram nodded. "I'll ask Mr. Gumplin to wait if you don't make it."

Jace nodded. "Thanks." He started to run. It was hard because everyone was going toward the busses. He had to zigzag, saying, "excuse me" about every two seconds. Finally, he got back to room 37. The door was closed and for a second Jace was afraid Mr. Hiss was gone for the day. He took a deep breath and tried the knob. To his relief, it turned and he pushed the door open slowly.

Mr. Hiss was in the room, still sitting at his desk. He was bent over something, his forehead almost touching the desk blotter.

"I came to get my math book, Mr. Hiss," Jace said politely. Mr. Hiss didn't seem to hear him. Jace hesitated. "I came to get my book. I forgot it," he repeated. Mr. Hiss bobbed his head up and down, but it didn't look like he was nodding. It was more like he was touching his nose to the desk.

Jace glanced back out into the hall. The crowds were thinned out now. In another few minutes the hallway would be empty. Jace started for his desk. He didn't want to miss the bus. Even with

Abram pleading with him, Mr. Gumplin would not wait very long.

Jace rummaged through the mess in his desk until he found his math book. Then he straightened and turned toward the door. Mr. Hiss was still hunched over his desk. Jace started feeling creepy again. What was wrong? Was Mr. Hiss sick or something?

Jace glanced back at Mr. Hiss and bumped into a desk. He stumbled, twisting to catch his balance. He dropped the math book and it fell flat, smacking the floor with startling loudness in the quiet room. Jace spun to apologize to Mr. Hiss, then he froze. Mr. Hiss had straightened abruptly and was looking at Jace. Jace sucked in a quick, frightened breath. Mr. Hiss's eyes were red—deep, ugly red—and slitted with vertical, cat's eye pupils. His heart thudding in his chest, Jace ran out of the classroom.

Every morning when Jace opened his eyes, he felt a little sick. He did not want to go to school. He didn't even really want to get up. First, he had to shake off the nightmares he kept having about Mr. Hiss. Then, all day long at school, everything went on as usual and everyone was talking about what a good teacher Mr. Hiss was. Even Molly. This morning was no different. Jace stretched and tried to think about something besides Mr. Hiss.

He and his dad had gone to play miniature golf on the weekend. He had actually forgotten about Mr. Hiss for a few hours. That had been fun. What wasn't fun was the way both his parents kept looking at him and asking him what was wrong. How could he explain?

"Jace? Are you up?" his mother yelled down the hall. Jace sat up and swung his legs out of the bed. He stood up and stared down at his bare feet on the carpet. His knees felt stiff and wooden as he walked to the closet and pulled out clothes.

"Jace?" His father sounded like he always did, cheerful and wide awake.

"I'm up," Jace called. His own voice sounded flat and strange. He kept looking out the window while he was putting on his shoes. It was going to be another beautiful day. Clear and cold, with the brilliant pale sunshine that only came in late fall.

Jace went downstairs and slid into his chair at the breakfast table. His mother was hanging up the phone.

"I just made an appointment for you," she said slowly. "With the school counselor."

Jace rolled his eyes, feeling even sicker. "I don't want to go see Mrs. Chandler."

His mother was shaking her head. "You're acting like something is wrong. You've been having bad dreams. I hear you getting up at night. Maybe it's something it'd be easier to talk to a counselor about. Is Brett picking on you again?"

Jace shook his head, half-standing, but his mother held up her hand.

"What are the dreams about?"

Jace shook his head again, but she didn't give up. "Well?"

"I dream about Mr. Hiss," he blurted out.

His mother looked surprised. "The substitute?"

He nodded. "He's creepy. One day after school when I had to go back for a book his eyes were red."

"Maybe he stayed up too late," Jace's father said, smiling.

"Another time he had blood all over his face and hands and then a second later it was gone," Jace added. It sounded stupid and he knew it, but he couldn't stop himself. "And Molly says he eats eyeballs for lunch."

His mother sighed. "All right. That's enough. I wish you wouldn't watch those scary movies over at Abram's house. I won't argue about this, Jace. Mrs. Chandler is expecting you. Go straight to her office when you get to school. She'll write you a tardy slip."

His father patted his shoulders as he walked to the sink. "Go see her, Jace. It can't hurt. If you're worried about grades or Mrs. Dement or something, she can help."

Jace shuffled his feet under the table. They were ignoring what he'd said, and he understood why. It didn't make any sense. He picked at his toast until it was time to go. Then he pulled on his jacket and got his backpack.

"I know you're fine, Jace," his mother said

when she hugged him good-bye. She touched his cheek and dropped into a heavy accent. "Thees eess zee best son in zee vurld. Just a leetle too much imageenation." Jace tried to grin at her. She smiled and hugged him. "See you after school."

Jace tried not to think about anything as he started toward the bus stop. It was getting colder. The sidewalks crackled with frost beneath his shoes. He kicked at a frozen clump of brown grass that had grown up through the cement.

"Hey, Jace!"

It was Abram, running toward him. Jace tried to smile at him. He hadn't told him about Mr. Hiss, and he still didn't want to. It all sounded so stupid. With every uneventful day that went past, it sounded sillier, even to himself. Maybe he had made it all up. What other explanation was there?

"Did you write the history assignment?" Abram asked when he got closer. Jace shook his head.

"It isn't due until this Friday."

Abram nodded and pushed his glasses up. I know. I just thought—"

"No," Jace repeated, interrupting him. "I haven't written it yet." His voice was sharp, angry.

Abram pushed at his glasses. His eyes shifted

from Jace's face to the sidewalk, then back. Jace felt like a jerk. Abram hadn't done anything.

"I had an argument with my parents this morning," Jace said into the silence. It was true, or at least partly true.

Abram scuffed at a thick patch of frost and let out a huge, plumed breath of steam. "I hate arguing with my mother."

Jace nodded. He looked up. The bus was only about three blocks away and he was grateful for the distraction. "We'd better hurry."

Without saying anything else, Abram started to run. Jace pounded along beside him, leaping over the curbs when they crossed the side streets. Mr. Gumplin didn't smile at them when he let them in. But then, Mr. Gumplin never smiled. Still, there were ways to tell when he was in a good mood. He didn't frown, and he actually said something that sounded like "Good Morning." Abram sang out an answer and grinned at Jace as they slid into a seat.

"Did you hear that?" he leaned close to whisper. "Gumplin must be having a wonderful day."

Jace tried to smile at the joke. The smile felt a little funny, like it was a few sizes too small. "I have to see the counselor this morning." Jace was surprised that he'd said it. He hadn't meant to.

39

Abram pushed his glasses up. "Your mother?"

Jace nodded and stared straight ahead. "I guess she's worried about me."

Abram shrugged. "My mother made me go once. Are your grades bad?" Jace made a sound that didn't mean anything. His grades weren't bad. He shrugged and sighed.

Abram seemed satisfied. "Don't feel bad. Almost everyone has to go at least once. Mrs. Chandler is pretty nice."

Jace settled back in his seat and watched the houses and the autumn-brown lawns stream past the window. He wished that it would snow. He was tired of the bright sun that wasn't warm enough to let you stay out long during the day. It just made you think that it was nice outside. Then you actually opened the door and found out it was freezing.

When the bus stopped at school, Jace got up slowly. "I'll meet you in the library if I get finished before the bell."

Abram looked at him and smiled. "It won't be so bad."

Jace turned without saying anything and headed for the office.

When he got there, Mrs. Chandler was waiting for him. She was a tall woman with iron gray hair and a big smile. Jace stared at her. She had at least twice as many teeth as anyone else. She chuckled, which made her smile sag a little, then it widened again. "So, how are you doing this morning?"

Jace followed her into her office and sat down. He didn't know what to say. He wondered what his mother had told her.

"Your mother told me," Mrs. Chandler began, as though she had read his mind, "that you seem upset. She thought that you might be under too much pressure over school. She told me you're a pretty serious student."

Jace nodded. He was a serious student. He tried hard to keep his grades high. He wanted to go to college. Mrs. Chandler smiled again. Jace could not stop staring at her face. She didn't have more teeth than other people, he decided, she just had bigger gums. Actually, she had bigger everything. She was huge. Jace realized that while he was staring at her, Mrs. Chandler was staring at him. Was he supposed to say something?

"Well, are you?"

"Am I what?" Jace answered.

Mrs. Chandler tapped at her desk with one fingertip. "Are you worried about school?"

Jace shook his head. Then he nodded. He wasn't worried about school. But he didn't want to explain what he was worried about.

Mrs. Chandler sat back, tapping her fingertip against the edge of her desk. "It's normal for someone your age to have a good imagination," she said quietly. Jace tensed. She couldn't know. How could she know? He looked out the window. There was that false bright sun, pretending like it was warm.

"Your mother tells me that frightening movies and TV shows scare you quite a bit." She paused, inspecting his face for a reaction. Then she went on. "I'm like that. Anything scary gives me nightmares." Mrs. Chandler continued watching him closely. Jace felt himself blushing. Mrs. Chandler reached out and touched his arm lightly. "It's nothing to be ashamed of. Frightening movies . . ."

Jace shook his head. "This doesn't have anything to do with movies."

Mrs. Chandler tapped silently at her desk. Then she raised her chin. "Your mother seemed to feel that perhaps your friend Abram has been talking you into watching movies that upset you. She says she thinks you're having nightmares."

"No," Jace said quickly. "Abram hasn't . . ."

"It wouldn't be anything that would get him in trouble, of course," Mrs. Chandler assured him.

Jace shook his head, refusing to look up. He stared at his shoes. The laces were getting so dirty that they were turning gray.

"Jace?" Mrs. Chandler's voice was soft and kind. "Jace, your mother seems like a very nice woman."

Jace looked up at her, astonished. Of course his mother was nice. What did that have to do with anything? He didn't want to go to class. He wanted to go home. Just then, the warning bell rang. Automatically, Jace started to get up, then sank back into his chair under the weight of Mrs. Chandler's unwavering gaze. She was tapping, tapping. "I looked at your records. I think that you just need to tell your mother whatever it is that's bothering you, and that you two can work everything out. If you feel like she pushes you too hard sometimes, you can tell her. I liked her when we spoke. She seemed like a very fair and good person."

Jace looked up and nodded, feeling numb. He found himself wanting to tell Mrs. Chandler what he'd seen. He wanted to tell his mother and Abram. But if he did, he'd spend the rest of his life in counselors' offices.

"Problems usually don't go away if we ignore them," Mrs. Chandler was saying. "We have to face what is bothering or scaring us."

Jace rubbed his hand across his eyes. Mrs. Chandler was right. He had been trying to ignore

43

what he had seen, to pretend it hadn't happened. And it wasn't working.

Jace sat up a little straighter. Maybe that was what he should do. Prove that he wasn't imagining things—or, he allowed himself to think, that he was. Either way, at least he could stop worrying and wondering. He took a deep breath, feeling better. "Can I go to class?"

Mrs. Chandler was still examining his face. Jace felt itchy, like she was tickling him with something.

"May I go to class?" he asked again, correcting his own grammar.

Mrs. Chandler stood up. "Yes. But if you have any other difficulties I want you to come see me. Do you understand? I can help if you're upset with something. Or talk to your mother. She seemed like a very nice person."

She is! Jace shouted inside his mind. My mother is a very nice person. He turned to the door and went out, without looking back. Mrs. Chandler was probably a very nice person, too. And she probably could help him if he were upset about something. In fact, she had helped him. He turned the corner and started down the long hallway that would take him to room 37. He felt a lot better. He wasn't confused anymore. He knew what he was going to do.

44

5

Jace spent every day in class watching Mr. Hiss very carefully. Apart from his weird voice and the way he over-pronounced every word, nothing seemed unusual. He was a good teacher. Every day in class they talked about the essay that they were supposed to write by Friday. Mr. Hiss tried to get everyone excited about the assignment—and almost everyone was. While he talked, his funny eyes seemed to bug out a little farther and his voice seemed to stretch like a rubber band. But nothing really odd happened. There was no hint of anything really strange.

By Wednesday, Jace began to think that nothing more was going to happen. Maybe the light in the little room had been red. Maybe he had somehow imagined Mr. Hiss's eyes being so strange in the classroom. Once or twice, Jace saw Mr. Hiss looking at him intently—or at least he thought he was. Maybe he was making that up, too. In any case, Mr. Hiss's eyes looked fine now—plain brown. His decision to prove what he'd seen wasn't going to help at all. Nothing strange was happening.

Thursday morning, Abram and Jace were late for the bus as usual. They ran while Mr. Gumplin waited, frowning. Sliding into the window seat, Jace silently promised himself that he would find some way to figure out whether or not he was imagining things before the day was over. "No matter what," he whispered aloud.

Abram was looking at him quizzically. "Talking to yourself? You've been acting funny this whole week." He grinned and Jace knew he was trying to be nice. Abram leaned closer. "You never told me about your appointment with Chandler. Was it awful or something?"

Jace shook his head. "No. It was . . . okay. You know."

Abram nodded. "I told you. It doesn't mean anything. She's nice."

Jace looked out the window. He didn't want to talk about Mrs. Chandler. He wanted to think of a way to find out about Mr. Hiss.

"I went over to her house once," Abram was saying. "Her daughter is a friend of my oldest sister. It was strange to see her like that."

Jace nodded absently, barely listening. "Like what?"

Abram shoved his glasses up. "In a bright pink swimming suit."

Jace focused on Abram's eyes. Mrs. Chandler in a swimming suit? He almost giggled. That was almost harder to imagine than the things he was so worried about. Jace blinked. He blinked again.

Abram was shaking his head slowly. "Yeah. It was amazing."

Jace could only nod.

"And she was laughing and goofing around. People are really different when they're at home."

Jace turned the idea over in his mind. It was true. His father did things at home that he never did anywhere else. He sometimes ate breakfast wearing only his socks and underwear, for instance. His mother sometimes put green clay stuff on her face and walked around looking like a dorkus until it dried. It was supposed to clean out her pores or something. Neither one of them would ever let anyone else see them doing things like that.

Jace closed his eyes, thinking. His mother sometimes yelled, got really loud and angry at silly things, like stubbing her toe or something. She got really goofy and silly sometimes, too.

Jace was positive that she never did that at work, or anywhere else.

Jace sat up straighter. He needed to be able to see Mr. Hiss at home. He needed to be able to see what he did when he was alone. Suddenly, Jace realized that Abram was looking at him.

"Are you all right?"

Jace nodded. "I'm fine." Jace pretended to look through his backpack. What did a man like Mr. Hiss do when he was alone with his family or closest friends? Maybe he didn't have a family. Maybe he wasn't even married. Maybe he was really a vampire, or werewolf or something. Jace shook his head. There had to be some explanation for the things that he had seen. He had to find out.

When they got to class, Mr. Hiss asked for their math homework. Jace took out his paper and passed it in with the others. Then he got out his math book. But he wasn't thinking about math. Jace spent math period making a list. While Mr. Hiss helped the kids who were still having trouble subtracting fractions, Jace was thinking furiously.

He would have to:
1. Find out where Mr. Hiss lived.
2. Figure out how to get there.

3. Find a way to see inside without getting arrested.
4. Find some way to prove whatever he saw—maybe pictures.

He would need:
1. A camera.
2. A good excuse for being late getting home.
3. Another appointment with Mrs. Chandler if he got caught.
4. Another place to live if his father found out.

Jace almost groaned out loud. He glanced up at Mr. Hiss. He looked so normal, writing problems on the blackboard. But he wasn't. Jace stared at the substitute. Or was he? Maybe all this was ridiculous. Jace sighed. If he had imagined everything, he was going to risk getting into a lot of trouble for nothing.

At noon recess, Abram wanted to play basketball. Jace tried to concentrate, but he played badly. He was too preoccupied. He couldn't seem to stop thinking of ways to find out where Mr. Hiss lived. He could come straight out and ask him, but that seemed pretty stupid. He could talk Abram or Molly or someone else into asking, but

49

that meant he would have to explain why or else make up a reason.

Jace saw Abram frowning at him.

"What?"

"You just let that pass go right by you," Abram accused him.

Jace shrugged. "Sorry."

Jace tried to play better as the game went on, but he kept dropping passes and he wasn't shooting well at all. Abram kept staring at him. Finally, the warning bell rang. As they walked back across the playground to return the ball to the PE room, Brett and Molly came up to them.

"Hiss isn't so bad after all," Brett said, squinting up at the pale sun.

Molly nodded, bouncing her hair. "I like him. Not as much as Mrs. Dement. But almost."

Jace turned to look at Abram. He was nodding.

Molly grinned. "It's a pretty neat history assignment, huh?"

Brett laughed. "When Molly likes homework, something is wrong."

Jace wanted to walk away, to be by himself, but he didn't want Abram worrying about him. He didn't want anyone else noticing either. So he stood there with the others, thinking about how he was going to find out where Mr. Hiss lived. He had to know. He had to find out what was going on. If anything was. He forced himself to smile, glancing at Abram. His friend was watching him closely.

Once they were back in the classroom, Mr. Hiss gave them some time to work on their history essays if they hadn't started them at home yet.

Jace had been putting it off, partly because he'd been so preoccupied. Now, he was grateful for something to take his mind off Mr. Hiss. He decided to pretend he was a silversmith's apprentice whose parents were loyal to the king, and that his master was a Revolutionary. In his essay, he wrote about being sent to buy supplies at the docks. Halfway home, a group of kids chased him, throwing rocks. His master saw them, but didn't help him.

Jace wrote the essay slowly, taking up all the time that he could. Even so, he finished before Mr. Hiss was ready. So he sat quietly, watching Mr. Hiss go through their homework papers.

At the end of the day, Jace told Abram to have Mr. Gumplin wait. Then he ran back to the classroom. Mr. Hiss was just on his way out. Jace hung back, pretending to fiddle with his books, then he followed. Mr. Hiss turned down the long hall toward the library.

Jace counted to twenty, then followed him into the library. Mr. Hiss was standing, talking to Ms.

51

Kosanovitch at her desk. They whispered, which was the only way that Ms. Kosanovitch allowed anyone to talk in her library. Jace pretended to be looking through the shelves, his heart racing. In another minute or two he was going to have to head for the bus. He strained to overhear what they were saying. Maybe there would be some clues he would follow if he could just hear them. But he couldn't. He was too far away and they were whispering.

Mr. Hiss suddenly straightened and turned. Jace spun around and walked quickly over to the far side of one of the bookshelves. Jace held his breath for a count of fifteen, then he risked another look. Mr. Hiss was standing up straight now, looking out the windows. Jace followed his gaze. Mrs. Chandler was unlocking her car just on the other side of the glass. Across the parking lot Jace saw Ms. Peery, his teacher from the year before, climbing into a white Jeep. As he stood there, Jace began to smile. Of course—the teachers' parking lot. He could come to the library every day after school, and he would start watching before school, too. One day he would have to get lucky. He would see Mr. Hiss driving up, or getting into his car to leave. Then he'd at least see which direction he lived in. Jace turned toward the library doors, and went back out into the pale sunshine. Halfway across the play-ground, he started to run.

As he climbed up the steps and slid into the seat beside Abram, Jace tried not to let his excitement show. It was going to take time to figure out exactly where Mr. Hiss lived. He would just have to be patient. It felt so good to be doing something.

Friday morning, Jace turned in his history assignment. He had copied it over from the rough draft he had done the day before, and he thought that it was pretty good. As Mr. Hiss collected the papers, he was looking around the room. His odd, buggy eyes flitted from one face to the next, as usual. When his eyes met Jace's, he smiled. Jace tried to smile back, but he couldn't. He thought that he saw Mr. Hiss shake his head before he looked away. Jace swallowed hard. He didn't want Mr. Hiss to realize that he was being watched.

Late in the afternoon, Mr. Hiss talked to the class about their next big assignment. "I'd like you to write about your day-to-day recreation," he said slowly, scanning their faces. He smiled. "What do you do for fun around here?"

"Like movies and parks and stuff?" someone asked from the back of the room.

Mr. Hiss nodded. "Exactly. Not big vacation ac-

53

tivities like skiing or camping. I mean things we do in our own neighborhood. We have miniature golf, for example. Or pizza places with arcades. Or maybe you like bike riding, or gardening. What do you like to do—just for the fun of it? Abram?"

Abram sat up straighter in his chair. "Miniature golf. That place up on Binks Street is fun."

Mr. Hiss nodded. "I like that one, too."

Jace listened intently as Mr. Hiss spoke. "So, Abram likes miniature golf. What else for fun?"

"Once it snows, we'll be able to sled," Molly said quietly. Jace turned to look at her, then turned back.

"I used to love to sled Morgan's Hill when I was your age," Mr. Hiss agreed, smiling. Jace drew in a quick breath. Morgan's Hill was only about ten blocks from his house. He let out his breath and raised his hand. Mr. Hiss nodded at him.

"Did you grow up around here?"

Mr. Hiss nodded. "The house I grew up in was down on Haller Ave. It was torn down for the mini-mall. But I can see Morgan's Hill from my back windows now, up on Garland Street." He shook his head. "You guys are making me feel old."

Everyone laughed. Jace saw Abram duck his head a little and knew that he was pushing up

54

his glasses. It was hard to keep from grinning, but Jace tried. He didn't want Mr. Hiss to notice a wide, silly smile on his face. He finally covered his mouth with his hand as though he were coughing or trying not to sneeze.

Garland Street! This was going to be easier than he had ever hoped. A lot easier. Garland Street was one of the oldest parts of his neighborhood. It was a dead end and it was only about five blocks long. And the way the hill ran, there were only four or five houses that could possibly have a view of Morgan's Hill and one of those was an old boarded up place. Jace folded his hands on his desk and stared at his fingers. This was it! Now all he had to do was find out what kind of car Mr. Hiss drove. Then he would look for the car in front of houses on Garland Street. His heart thudding, Jace leaned forward and whispered to Abram that he had a library book to return after school. Then he sat back and waited for the bell to ring.

They hurried to the library after the final bell and Abram stood impatiently by the door while Jace set his backpack on a table by the windows. Jace glanced out. He could only hope that Mr. Hiss would show up before he had to head for the bus. He rifled through his papers, muttering.

"We'd better get going," Abram whispered from the doorway.

Jace looked up. "Right. We will in a minute." He glanced out the window. Mr. Hiss was on the sidewalk!

"Come on, Jace." Abram was fidgeting. "Gumplin won't wait if neither of us shows up on time. He'll think one of our mothers picked us up."

Jace rummaged through his backpack again, glancing out the window. Mr. Hiss was crossing the parking lot now. Jace looked at Abram. "I know it's in here." He pawed through his books. Then he glanced out the window again. Mr. Hiss was standing beside a little red VW. He took a set of keys out of his pocket. Jace exhaled and pulled the library book out of his pack.

"Here it is." He smiled and slid the book onto the check-in counter. Then he turned to Abram. "Let's go."

He shot one last glance out the window. Mr. Hiss had opened the car door and walked around to open the trunk. He looked up and scanned the parking lot like a criminal in a movie. Jace could feel Abram's curious stare, but he continued to watch Mr. Hiss through the window. Jace caught his breath. There was something in the trunk of the car. It looked furry, and huge, like a bear, or maybe some other kind of animal.

56

"Jace, let's go."

Jace glanced at Abram, then back out the window. Mr. Hiss was leaning into the trunk, bending low enough to bring his face close to the whatever-it-was. Jace strained to see, but the angle of sight was all wrong. Mr. Hiss's back blocked his view.

"Come on," Abram hissed at him. Ms. Kosanovitch cleared her throat across the room and Jace looked at her. She was frowning, staring at him. He looked back out the window. Mr. Hiss had closed the trunk and was sliding into the driver's seat. Jace shivered and turned back to Abram.

Early Saturday morning, Jace awoke and stared at the ceiling. Today he would find out where Mr. Hiss lived. All he had to do was ride his bike up to Garland Street and look for the little red VW he'd seen Mr. Hiss get into. It was going to be easy. Garland Street was a dead end, and most of the houses were old with huge yards and big shade trees. There was an old Victorian house that had been abandoned for years where the street ended. He would be able to hide in the bushes that lined its rutted driveway if he had to. It would be a perfect place to watch from if Mr. Hiss lived in one of the last houses.

Jace sat up and swung his feet to the floor. He felt good. Today he was going to start doing something, instead of just worrying and wondering. He started to hum as he went downstairs. His parents were in the kitchen. They were doing what they usually did on Saturday mornings. His mother was reading the newspaper. His father was making breakfast. Jace slumped into a chair and yawned.

His mother ruffled his hair. "Good morning. Abram called earlier. He wants you to go bike riding." Jace hesitated. Then he made a quick decision and nodded at his mother. He was glad that Abram had called. All he was going to do today was figure out which house was Mr. Hiss's. It wouldn't hurt to have Abram along—in fact it would make things more fun.

His mother smiled. "Call him back if you want to go. He called almost an hour ago. He'll give up on you."

"Hurry up," his father said, turning away from the stove. "World famous scrambled eggs are almost ready."

Jace jumped up and ran to the phone in the hall. He punched the buttons, then waited as the phone rang six or seven times. Abram's family never hurried to grab the phone. Abram still wanted to ride and they agreed to meet in half an hour. Jace slid back into his chair just as his father set a steaming plate in front of him.

"Don't rush. Eat slowly enough to taste it."

Jace looked up and grinned. "I'll try." It was a joke between him and his father. It seemed like he was hungry all the time lately. His mother said it was because he was growing so fast. Jace lifted a piece of toast and took a small bite. His father nodded approvingly. The instant he looked away, Jace crammed the rest of the toast into his mouth and took a drink of milk. Then he started in on the scrambled eggs. Every time his father looked at him, he chewed slowly and nodded his head appreciatively. His father laughed.

"Your mother has her theater group meeting, and I have a few errands. We'll be back in a couple hours, but take your key just in case." Jace nodded and finished his eggs.

When Abram knocked, Jace was almost ready. He went to get his bike from the backyard while Abram pedalled around in a slow circle at the end of the driveway. The sun was pale gold again, bright without heat. Jace coasted toward Abram, who looked up and grinned.

"Where do you want to go?"

Jace wrinkled his brow, as though he had to think about it. "Up to Garland Street? It has that neat hill."

Abram swung in one more circle, cutting it tighter this time. "Fine with me."

Jace nodded and pedalled off, standing up to build up some speed. He crossed Porter Street, careful to watch for cars. Abram was right behind

60

him. They rode single file until they turned the corner onto Brace Street. Then Jace slowed as Abram came up beside him. Brace Street had a wide paved shoulder that all the kids used as a bike lane. There wasn't much traffic on Saturday, either.

"Good day to ride."

Jace nodded, glancing at Abram. It was a good day to ride, but that wasn't what he was thinking about. Jace took a deep breath and stood up again to pedal hard. "Race you to Garland."

Abram shouted an acceptance and they were off. Jace's quick decision to race had won him a small lead. Abram was a good bike rider, but they were better matched than they were at running. Jace rode his hardest, pushing himself until his lungs burned. As he signalled and leaned into the corner, turning onto Garland Street, he was still ahead of Abram. He sat up and coasted, slowing down. Behind him, Abram screamed and pretended to beat his head against his handlebars. "You won, you jerk! How could you actually beat me?"

Jace laughed as they slowed almost to a stop, heaving plumes of breath into the crisp air. Then his laugh died in his throat. He stared up the street, still panting. He felt sick. He had imagined a lot of different things happening, but somehow this had never occurred to him. The red VW was coming toward them. Mr. Hiss was on his way somewhere. Abruptly, Jace angled toward the edge of the road, turning his head a little. He didn't want Mr. Hiss to recognize him.

"Hey," Abram called from behind him. "That's Mr. Hiss. That's our sub."

"Don't look at him," Jace commanded. "Don't let him see who we are."

"Why not?" Abram shouted, but Jace shook his head furiously. Abram nodded and Jace turned to face away from the street, slowing his bike. He glanced back once to see that Abram had stopped his bike and was pretending to bend down to tie his shoe, just as the red VW puttered past them. Jace kept his head turned until the sound of the little engine faded away. Then he exhaled. If Mr. Hiss had recognized them, he hadn't slowed down or called to them.

Jace pulled in a deep breath as the little car turned the corner and headed down Brace Street.

"What are you doing?" Abram demanded.

Jace frowned. It was Saturday. Mr. Hiss was probably gone for the rest of the day. He might be gone for the rest of the weekend. Everything was ruined.

Jace realized that he hadn't answered Abram's question. He looked up. "I just didn't want him to see us, that's all. I didn't want him to know that we live around here."

Abram shook his head. "Why? What do we have to hide? Or were you planning on burning down his house or something?" He squinched his eyes shut and worked his jaw and his eyebrows. It was a great face, like a deranged fire-starter.

Jace laughed. "Sure. That's it. I always wanted to burn down a house."

Abram looked at him for a second. "You sure are acting weird lately."

Jace shrugged. "I know. I'll explain it when I can."

"Race you to the end of Garland Street," Abram said suddenly. He leapt onto his bike and coasted a few feet, then stood up and pedalled furiously.

Jace was caught completely by surprise. He circled around and stood up on his pedals, but his right foot slipped and he nearly went down. He glanced up. Abram was already way ahead because the street went downhill all the way to the end. Jace grimaced. Abram was going to win by a mile, but he still had to try. Jace shoved his weight down on the pedals, finding a rhythm and gritting his teeth until his bike was flying down the hill.

Jace looked ahead. The street ended at the driveway of the old abandoned house. It had a wide, shrub-lined driveway that they sometimes used to turn around in, but usually they just stayed in the street. There was something spooky about the house. It was so old that the maple trees around it were huge, their branches almost touching the ground. As long as Jace could remember, it had been boarded shut. On Halloween the older boys always dared each other to go in, but Jace didn't think anyone ever really had. He wouldn't, that was for sure. The house was creepy.

Abram's victory yell brought Jace out of his thoughts. He frowned. It was hard enough losing to Abram when they ran. On bikes, it was worse because he knew that he could win. He felt like pounding his handlebars and screaming. He bit his lip instead. He wasn't going to be a lousy sport. Abram never was.

Jace grinned determinedly as Abram swung out of his wide turnaround circle and came back toward him. Abram grinned back. Then his expression changed. He raised his hands off his handlebars and made a swirling, pointing gesture. Jace braked and craned his head around to look.

The red VW was coming around the corner of Brace and Garland. It was coming straight toward them again. Jace jerked his head back and shouted to Abram. "Let's hide in there." He pointed toward the brushy drive.

Abram looked reluctant but he nodded and swung his bike back around.

Jace stood up on his pedals again and shoved downward with each foot, forcing his tired muscles to work hard. He entered the driveway just behind Abram. They rode furiously, the gritty soil ticking against their spokes. When the driveway started to narrow, Jace braked and put his right foot down. He spun his bike in a half-circle and watched as Abram braked hard, then swung around in a tight arc.

Jace smiled. But Abram didn't smile back. He lifted his right hand and pointed. "Oh, no, Jace."

Jace followed his gesture and almost groaned out loud. Through the bushy tunnel of the drive, he could see the red VW was still coming straight toward them, slowing as it neared the end of Garland Street. Jace watched, transfixed. The little red car wasn't turning to either side. It wasn't going up any of the driveways. It took him a few seconds to understand.

When he did, Jace leapt off his bike and rammed it against the tangle of untrimmed bushes. A second later Abram was beside him. They shoved their bikes forward, digging their feet into the pebbly soil. Twigs began to shatter and Jace managed to roll his bike forward. He ducked his head and pushed harder, glancing up once to see that Abram had managed to get his bike into the bushes, too. Jace took another step. Then two more. He looked back at the driveway, then at Abram. His friend was less than fifteen feet from him, but he could barely see his face through the thicket of leaves and branches.

"We're okay," Abram said quietly. "No one could see us in this junk."

Jace nodded, putting a finger to his lips. The VW engine sounded like a sewing machine tapping smoothly toward them. The sound got louder. Then, suddenly, the red VW was there, rolling past them on the narrow road they had just left. Jace could see the side of Mr. Hiss's face for a second. He was frowning, but he didn't look left or right. Jace exhaled slowly. He hadn't seen them, then. The little car passed them, then was gone, puttering on toward the old boarded up house.

"What do you think he's doing here?" Abram whispered.

Jace shrugged. "Maybe he's lost or something."

Abram shook his head in wonder. "Or maybe he lives here?" He jerked a thumb in the direction of the old house.

Jace shook his head immediately, then stopped

himself. "It's possible, I guess. I would never have thought to look here."

Abram pushed up his glasses. "Look here?" He stared at Jace. "Look here for what?"

Jace stared at his bike seat for a minute, rocking back and forth on his feet. Then he looked up and saw the look of concern on Abram's face. "I just wondered where Mr. Hiss lived, that's all."

Abram raised his eyebrows and turned to look toward the house. He stood still and was silent. Jace listened, too. The sound of the VW had died away. Mr. Hiss had turned the car off. Did he live here then? How could anyone live in a house that had all its windows broken or boarded up, the remaining glass opaque with dust and cobwebs? Why would anyone want to try? He shook his head and met Abram's eyes. "Have you heard anyone talking about someone moving in here?"

Abram lifted his shoulders. "No. But there's only little kids on this street since the Gallagers moved to Idaho. So maybe no one has noticed yet."

He nodded slowly. He stood absolutely still for a few seconds, concentrating. There was no sound from the direction of the house. Not even voices. He pushed his bike back toward the road, feeling the dig and slap of branches this time. Abram freed his bike too and they stood, looking at each other without speaking for a long time.

"Well," Jace said finally. "Maybe I'll just try to sneak up and see if he really lives here."

Abram shook his head instantly and kept shaking it as he spoke. "No. That's a terrible idea. You could get into trouble. And besides, who cares? I don't even understand why we're sneaking around like this. Mr. Hiss wouldn't care if he saw us. He probably wouldn't even recognize us. Subs never really figure out who's who."

Jace bit his lip. "Well," he said finally, "I guess I was just curious. No one has ever lived here, have they?"

Abram glanced up the driveway. It was impossible to see the house from where they stood. The road curved, and the trees were as thick as a forest.

Jace watched him for a minute. "You don't have to come."

Abram twisted his foot in the dirt. "I don't think you should. What if he does get mad? He could flunk you. Your parents would be furious."

Jace frowned. He hadn't even thought about that. He didn't think it was true that Mr. Hiss could flunk him, but maybe it was. But why would Mr. Hiss get mad? He hadn't even brought the camera, because he hadn't wanted to explain things to Abram. He could just say he was lost or something. Besides, Mr. Hiss wasn't even going to see him. He looked at Abram. "I won't get caught."

Abram scuffed his shoe again. "I don't think you should."

Jace tightened his grip on his handlebars. He might be the one who didn't like scary movies, but Abram was more afraid than he was right now. Of course, Abram had no idea what he needed to find out. Or why. Jace smiled at his friend. "It's okay, Abram. I don't even want you to go up there with me."

Abram exhaled in relief. "You don't?"

Jace shook his head. "No. But will you wait out there?" He pointed down the driveway out to the sunny street. "Back on Garland?"

Abram nodded eagerly. "Sure. Of course. I won't leave until you come back out."

Jace reached out and slugged Abram gently on the shoulder. "Okay. I won't be very long."

Abram nodded and swung his leg over his bike seat. "I'll be up across from where the Gallagers used to live."

"Thanks," Jace said, meaning it. He knew that Abram would wait until next Tuesday if that's what it took. Smiling at Abram once more to hide

69

his own nervousness, Jace waited and watched as he pedalled away. Then he backed his bike off the road, pushing it through the same narrow slot in the brush he had just left. The sound of the rasping branches seemed unbelievably loud. Once he was sure that his bike was well concealed, Jace worked his way around it and back to the road. He glanced out toward Garland Street. Abram was already out of sight.

Jace took a deep breath and started walking. His knees felt strange. He closed his eyes for a second, and without meaning to, he remembered Mr. Hiss's face in the little room of the library. He shivered, but he forced himself to keep walking.

7

Jace walked fast until the road straightened and he could see the house. Then he slowed down, keeping to the edge of the bushes. The VW was parked near the rear of the house, and a screen door stood open onto the wide front porch. He stopped and stood still, leaning back into the bushes.

The old Victorian house still looked spooky and old, but the windows had been fixed. There was fresh paint on the porch, too. And someone had cleaned out the flower beds next to the porch. The raked beds looked smooth and ready to plant. Was Mr. Hiss a gardener? Roses and violets? Jace inhaled slowly. Maybe he had imagined everything. It would sure be simpler if he had. He could just make another appointment with Mrs. Chandler and ... There was a sound from inside the house.

Jace leaned forward, trying to see into the big window that faced the driveway. But the angle was wrong for this time of day. The mid-morning sun glinted back at him, brilliant and heatless. Another sound from inside the house made him jump. It began with a heavy thudding, then escalated into a high-pitched whining sound. Jace took a step or two forward, then hesitated. A blender? The whining sound died. He took another few steps, walking so closely to the edge of the driveway that the bushes tore at his clothing. The door on the porch banged open and Jace caught his breath and ducked down as Mr. Hiss appeared. He was carrying something, a plate or a shallow bowl. Jace pressed himself back into the bushes.

Mr. Hiss was singing to himself as he carefully set the bowl on the porch railing. He poked at the contents with his finger, stirring them in slow circles. Jace strained to see. Mr. Hiss lifted a finger and licked the tip. He smiled and sang a little louder.

It all looked so normal that Jace began to feel silly. He was spying on a man who was about to sit on his porch and eat lunch. As he watched, Mr. Hiss pulled a hand towel from his back pocket and wiped his hands. Jace could see reddish stains from tomato sauce or something on

72

it. He sighed. Now Mr. Hiss was singing so loudly that Jace could have shouted and he wouldn't have heard him.

Jace started forward, inching his way along. He wasn't sure what he was doing—why he thought that he needed to get closer. After all, there was nothing to see except a bowl of spaghetti or ravioli or something.

Mr. Hiss turned abruptly and went back into the house, leaving the bowl on the porch railing. Jace could hear him singing inside. There was a little pause and then Mr. Hiss started another song. This one had a high part and he strained his voice, half-laughing, to get through the verse. The voice came closer, and Jace ducked down again, crouching behind the bushes. But Mr. Hiss didn't appear through the porch door. He started the second verse. It sounded as though he were still in the front of the house, but away from the door—probably in the room that had the big window. The sun still shone against the glass, but Jace squinted, trying to see through it anyway. He leaned forward, his eyes watering.

Mr. Hiss changed songs again. This time he was belting out a strange, off-key version of "Deck the Halls." Jace frowned. It wasn't even Thanksgiving yet. Mr. Hiss trilled the "falalalala lalalala" part and Jace almost laughed aloud.

Then Mr. Hiss's voice got softer, more distant. Was he going into another room, farther toward the back of the house? Jace stood up and swayed on his feet. He made his hands into fists and then released them slowly. If he was going to try to get closer, now was the time.

Mr. Hiss's singing got fainter, as though he had closed a door. Now. Now! Jace jerked into a run, stumbling a little in his nervousness. He sprinted up to the porch, then broke his stride, looking around wildly. There wasn't really anywhere to hide this close to the house. The planters had been cleared of the years of dead vines and bushes that had been piled high around the foundation. Jace looked desperately up at the porch. Mr. Hiss's bowl was still sitting on the rail. Impulsively, Jace reached up. In one smooth motion he swung onto the railing, looked into the bowl, then dropped back down to the ground.

For a second he just stared at the raked dirt beneath his feet, unable to move at all. His thoughts moved slowly, like helium balloons responding to a slight breeze. They seemed to tangle, then they separated and he could tell them apart again. There were three separate thoughts. The first was, Molly Grover was right. The second was, he might see me. And the third was this: that isn't spaghetti.

Jace turned to run. His breath was coming so quickly that he felt almost dizzy until his muscles used up the extra oxygen he was taking in. He was running so fast that he passed the place where he had hidden his bike and had to turn, trembling, to run back for it. Once he was on his bike, he wobbled so much that he was sure that he was going to fall before he could pedal out of the long, rutted driveway. Just as he cleared the last of the bushes, Abram rode up to him, his face tense and worried. "What happened, Jace? Did he see you?"

Jace could hear the ticking grind of the sandy dirt beneath their tires. "No. I . . . let's go. Let's get out of here."

Abram glanced past him anxiously. "Why? Is he chasing you?"

Jace shook his head again. "No." He pulled in a long shuddering breath. "No. I just want to go. Now."

Abram raised his eyebrows but he swung his bike around and started up the hill, glancing back three or four times until he seemed to be sure that Jace was coming. Then he rode harder.

Jace felt so shaky that he nearly stopped twice before they finally made it up the long sloping hill to Brace Street. He tried to smile when

Abram slowed to turn and look at him, but he couldn't.

Abram frowned again. "Are you sure you're all right?" he called out.

Jace nodded, and then kept nodding. Abram dropped back to ride beside him, glaring. "No you aren't. What happened?"

Jace slowed, then put his foot down and stopped altogether. He heard the squeak of Abram's brakes, but he didn't look up to meet his friend's eyes. He looked at the ground, toeing a pebble, pushing it from side to side. Then he looked at Abram. "Mr. Hiss isn't normal. Or I'm not."

Abram pushed up his glasses. "What do you mean?"

"I keep seeing things that don't make any sense."

Abram's frown deepened. Jace looked up at the sky to avoid Abram's eyes. "Mr. Hiss had a big bowl of eyeballs for lunch."

"What?" Abram almost yelled the word, and his voice was shrill.

Jace flinched. "I know it sounds impossible. Maybe it is."

"But you saw . . ." Abram asked, hesitating.

Jace nodded. "Yes."

Abram pushed up his glasses. "Through the

window? You probably saw something else and thought that it was—"

"No," Jace interrupted him. "Not through the window. Outside, on the porch rail. He went back in for a minute and he left the bowl out there. I saw them. I saw . . . I almost put my face in the bowl."

Abram shivered. "Maybe they're for some science project or something. My older sister saw a cow's eyeball in her science class once."

Jace nodded slowly, his hopes rising. "Maybe. Maybe that's what they were for. But . . ." he trailed off, shaking his head. He looked at Abram without saying anything else for a long time. Then he started talking again, describing what he had seen in the library, and how Mr. Hiss's eyes had been red and cat-like the day he'd forgotten his book.

"Wow," Abram breathed when he was finally finished. "Wow."

Jace looked out over the neighborhood. If Abram told his mother, there'd be a counselor's appointment Monday and probably another one the next day and another one after that.

"Let's go back," Abram said abruptly.

Jace shook his head. "We have to," Abram insisted. "We have to know." He shook his head.

"It does sound pretty strange, Jace. But remember what Molly said?"

Jace rested his head on his handlebars for a second. Then he looked up. "I remember. I thought it was just some stupid story."

Abram nodded quickly, like he was agreeing with his own thoughts, not with anything that Jace had said. "Come on." He pushed off and turned in a wide arc, heading back down Brace toward Garland. Jace watched him go for a minute, then turned his own bike around.

"Are you all right?" Abram called out as they let themselves gain speed going down the Garland Street hill. Jace nodded, but he couldn't say anything. His mouth was dry and the truth was that he was not all right. He was scared. But he wanted to go back, so he set his jaw and forced himself to pedal. More than anything he wanted Abram to see that bowl of eyeballs. He wanted someone he trusted to tell him that he wasn't making all this up.

They hid their bikes in the bushes near the end of the drive, then walked toward the house, jumping every time a bird rustled the leaves. Finally, they were standing in the bushes nearest the house. Jace was shivering as he pointed toward the bowl that was still there, still on the porch rail.

Abram nodded somberly, then leaned close to whisper. "Do you think he's still inside?"

Jace tilted his head, listening. "He was singing before, so I could tell. I don't hear him, now."

At that moment, the porch door banged open again. Jace flinched, pulling Abram down with him. They crouched behind the bush and peered through the twigs. Mr. Hiss came out of the house. He walked to the bowl and lifted it, peering at the contents. "Not bad," he said aloud. "Not bad at all." He stirred the contents with his finger, then licked it as he set the bowl back on the rail. Abram made a little sound of disgust. Mr. Hiss smiled to himself and went back inside.

"Go," Jace whispered urgently. "Just look and run back. Hurry."

Abram glanced at the house, then back at Jace. He jumped up and sprinted for the porch. Once he was close enough he pulled himself up on the rail, doing a chin-up while he scrabbled for a hold with his feet. Finally he braced himself so that he could straighten up and look down into the bowl. Jace watched as his friend's face went white. The porch door creaked and Abram's head jerked toward it. He dropped to the ground. He hit it running, and a second later he was beside Jace—both of them sprinting up the driveway. They stayed close to the inside edge of the curve, the bushes whipping their arms and legs. No one called out behind them and Jace began to hope they were in the clear. They pulled their bikes from the bushes and got on, wordlessly, and pedalled hard back down the sandy road.

They were all the way up the Garland Street hill, making the turn back onto Brace when Abram finally spoke.

"There's nothing wrong with you," he told Jace, shaking his head. "You aren't imagining anything."

Abram had to go visit his aunt with his parents on Sunday, so he made Jace promise not to go back up to the old Victorian house alone. So Jace spent the day playing catch with his father and helping his mother pull last year's cornstalks out of the garden. He found himself wishing that Monday morning would never come, that he would never have to go to school again.

When Monday morning came anyway, Jace met Abram on the sidewalk. On the bus, they sat close together, leaning down so that no one could hear them.

"I don't know if he is actually dangerous," Abram was saying. "All I know is that he is not normal. No science teacher would lick his fingers like that, or smile like that."

Jace nodded. "And why would he be smearing

blood on himself, and what about his eyes that time . . ."

"Maybe he's an alien," Abram whispered. "I mean, maybe . . . ?"

Jace nodded, feeling his stomach lurch as the bus lumbered over a bump. "Maybe. That's something I never thought about."

"What other explanation is there?"

Jace lifted his head. No one was looking at them. Everyone else thought that this was just a normal, happy Monday. The pale winter sun was shining into the bus windows. The older kids at the next stop were playing tag football to warm up. Jace ducked back down, but he couldn't think of anything else to say. He just stared at the floor, feeling uneasy. Abram smelled like toothpaste and wet wool.

"Well?" Abram demanded after a few seconds had gone by in silence. "What else could it be? He's someone who collects cows' eyeballs?"

Jace shook his head, feeling terrible. "Maybe they weren't cow's eyeballs."

Abram made a sound of disgust. "They had to be. They were too big to be . . . human." He whispered the last word, then glanced up and out the window, then back at Jace.

Jace shrugged miserably. "I think that we should just call the police."

82

Abram nodded. Then he shook his head. "I don't think so. There's no law against having laboratory specimens. And we don't even have proof of that."

Jace glanced out the window again. They were still on Brace Street, coming up to Garland. There weren't any school age kids on the street now, so there wasn't a bus stop. As Jace looked down the hill, the little red VW emerged from the brush-choked driveway. He touched Abram's shoulder and pointed. Abram stared out the window with him.

"How can an alien get a driver's license?"

Jace shook his head. Abram leaned back, his eyes meeting Jace's for a second. "You have to show them your birth certificate. Like vaccinations. I know. My sister got her license last summer."

"Then he couldn't have done it," Jace said slowly. "So he isn't an—"

"He could be," Abram said, raising his voice. "You can get fake birth certificates. Spies do it." Abram was no longer whispering. In fact, he was almost shouting.

"Shhhh." Jace glanced around. He was glad he'd told Abram, but he didn't want anyone else to know.

Abram looked sheepish and dropped his voice.

"Sorry. But there's just no other explanation that makes sense. Is there?"

Jace looked out the window again. He couldn't see the red VW anymore. "I don't know. I wish I did."

"Well, we'll watch him from now on. And the minute he does anything that could hurt someone we'll call the police."

Jace nodded, feeling a little better. He was glad that he had told Abram. He settled back into the bus seat and let himself relax. Worrying wouldn't help anything.

The morning was routine, or as routine as any day would ever be with Mr. Hiss. He held a spelling contest. Molly Grover won, and a boy named Seth Levin came in second. Hailey Hannah placed third. Abram came in fourth.

"But I could have done better," he told Jace at lunch. "I was too busy watching Mr. Hiss. He really is weird." They were outside, and Jace was leaning against the wall of the gym. The sun had warmed the bricks a little and it felt good. He nodded so that Abram would know he was listening, but he really didn't have anything to say. Mr. Hiss was weird-looking. And he did weird things. And Jace was sick of having to think about it.

"I think that we should go tell Mr. Franklin.

If there's two of us, they can't just say our imaginations are too good."

Jace thought about it for a second. Then he nodded slowly. Mr. Franklin was the principal. And he was fair. Even kids who didn't like him thought he was pretty fair. Maybe, Jace thought, they could at least get Mr. Franklin to start watching Mr. Hiss. It made sense. "Let's do it, Abram." He pushed off the wall and stood, looking at his friend. Abram nodded.

Together, they crossed the playground. Jace pushed open the heavy hall doors and they started walking. Jace heard the heavy door click into place behind them. The hallway was empty and their footsteps echoed a little.

They had to stand in line at the office. One girl had lost her coat. Another had lost a book. There was a boy who had forgotten his absence note. Then it was their turn.

"We want to see Mr. Franklin," Jace said as steadily as he could. The office was too bright and too busy. He swallowed.

The lady behind the counter smiled at him. "And what do you need to talk to the principal about, young man?" Her hair was almost blue. Her eyes were blue too, but darker. She was wearing a glittery bead necklace.

"I . . . we just want to talk to him," Jace repeated.

"And what is this concerning?" the woman asked.

Jace shook his head, feeling helpless. He didn't want to explain anything to her. Abram pushed up from behind him.

"Can't we just see Mr. Franklin? Please?" Jace watched Abram shove his glasses farther up his nose. His face was flushed, like he had a fever.

"Well, I am sorry, but you can't," the blue-haired woman said gently. "He's gone for two weeks. Mr. Hiss is acting as substitute principal."

Jace sank backward, his eyes stinging. He heard Abram make a little sound of despair.

"Is something wrong?" the woman asked. "Mr. Hiss is the substitute teacher for Mrs. Dement's class. He's had some administrative experience as well, so the school board thought he could handle both jobs for a little bit." She looked from Abram's face to Jace's, then back, frowning. "He was in earlier this morning, organizing things. Seems very capable. I'm sure he could handle anything that you—"

"No," Abram nearly shouted. Then he cleared his throat and managed to get his voice under control. "Ah, no." He cleared his throat a second time. "Thanks very much," he said in a normal tone. He glanced at Jace.

"Thanks," Jace said to the woman, pulling at Abram's arm. "Thanks so much." He pulled again and Abram almost fell backward into the kids lined up behind them. The woman was looking at them closely. Too closely.

Jace spun Abram around and held his arm as they left the office. The warning bell rang.

"Well, that was just a great idea," Abram moaned as they started back toward room 37. "Great."

Jace took a deep breath, then let it out. "Well. It was. How could you know?"

Abram took off his glasses and polished them on his shirt as they walked. "It feels like everything is wrong, doesn't it?"

Jace nodded. "Uh-huh."

The warning bell rang.

"We should hurry," Abram said in a dull voice. They walked a little faster without talking. At room 37, they turned in, exchanging an unhappy glance as they slid into their desks.

"We have something exciting this afternoon," Mr. Hiss announced from the front of the room. The class quieted as the tardy bell rang. Jace noticed a young woman sitting in a chair next to Mr. Hiss's desk. She was pretty. She had thick blonde hair cut bluntly into bangs across her forehead.

"My friend, Ms. Seale, has agreed to help me with a makeup demonstration that I think will interest you all," Mr. Hiss said. Jace saw some of the girls sit up straighter, curious. The rest of the kids just sat still, looking surprised. Most of the boys sat back in their chairs. Makeup? Jace shook his head. Mr. Hiss thought makeup would interest them? Everybody except the girls who wore lip gloss would be bored in ten minutes.

Abram turned and looked at Jace. His eyebrows were arched up higher than his glasses. "If she's his friend maybe she's creepy too?" He barely breathed the words so that only Jace could hear him. Then he slid back around in his seat.

"You're going to like this," Mr. Hiss was saying. "Darlene is very good." The young woman smiled up at Mr. Hiss and he smiled back at her. She tossed her head and her hair swung back and forth against her cheek.

I won't like it, Jace thought. I'll be too busy worrying. So will Abram. He couldn't even win the spelling contest like he should have been able to. It's because of you, he accused silently, staring at Mr. Hiss. For the first time, Jace felt angry instead of scared. It was an uncomfortable feeling, but it was an improvement.

88

Ms. Seale stood and faced the class. "Would you like to learn something about the makeup they use in movies? You know that young actors sometimes play old characters. Makeup can make them look the right age. Or sometimes actors play characters who aren't even human."

A murmur ran through the classroom. Everyone sat up a little straighter. Ms. Seale smiled at them. She pulled a big wooden box off the floor and slid it onto Mr. Hiss's desk. She flipped the latches and opened it. It had shelves built inside that hinged back, like a fisherman's tackle box. Jace could see false noses and dozens of little bottles and jars. "Who wants to be an alien from outer space?" Ms. Seale asked in a bright voice.

Abram jerked around, frowning.

"It's just makeup," Jace hissed back. But his stomach was tight. He felt like getting up and running out of the room. This was just too much. After everything that he and Abram had talked about, this was just too strange.

"I will," Molly Grover said from her desk near the door. She stood up. Ms. Seale motioned for her to come to the front of the room. Mr. Hiss stood and went to get another chair from the study table.

"Now," Ms. Seale said as Molly settled into a chair facing her. "Can everyone see? If you can't, you might want to move around. But everyone must be quiet and polite, please. Just find a spot where you can watch." Her heavy blonde hair fell over her brow and swung along her jawline as she talked. There was something odd-looking about her, Jace thought. She was smiling but the expression looked odd on her features, like it didn't belong there. Jace pushed the thought away. His imagination was getting out of hand. Before he knew it, he would be wondering about everyone he met.

Molly looked nervous. Jace stared at her. She would be twice as nervous if she had any idea what Abram thought about Mr. Hiss. Suddenly, Abram slid around in his seat again. "I wouldn't be Molly for anything."

Jace squirmed in his chair, nodding. Abram turned back. Ms. Seale was talking about how even the basic shape of someone's face could be changed with makeup. She tied a bib around Molly's neck like a barber. "This will keep the makeup from ruining Molly's clothes," she explained. She smiled brightly at the class, then looked back at Molly, her face becoming serious and intent.

Jace shifted in his desk. Ms. Seale seemed so bright and nice. She was pretty, with that beautiful, thick blonde hair and pink cheeks. How could she be dangerous? Yet he couldn't stop thinking that something was strange about her.

"You can start with a perfectly pretty face like Molly's," Ms. Seale explained, "and end up with an ugly space monster." Two or three people laughed and Molly giggled.

With quick motions, Ms. Seale spread a thick liquid over Molly's cheeks and forehead. Then she took soft plastic forms out of her case and began sticking them to Molly's face. One went across her eyebrows, and all the way up to her hairline. Two more were attached just below her cheek-bones. It just looked silly at first, like plastic lumps. But then Ms. Seale started putting flesh-colored putty, and then makeup onto Molly's skin, blending the plastic shapes in. Then she began adding colors.

Her hands moved so quickly that it was like watching magic. First Molly's skin turned bluish. Then blue-greenish. There were strange dark shadows under her eyes that made her cheeks look caved-in and hollow just above the unnatural bulges caused by the plastic forms.

Jace pulled in a startled breath. He would never have known that Molly was under the makeup. He could have seen her in a movie and he would have never recognized her at all. He

91

could sit twenty feet away from her like this and not recognize her.

"It's amazing, isn't it?" Mr. Hiss said in his too-careful voice. Ms. Seale smiled up at him and took a small paint brush out of her case. She began painting scale-like marks across Molly's forehead. She leaned close to Molly's face, concentrating, her brow furrowed.

Abram had been silent and still for a long time, watching. Now he turned around in his seat. His face was pale. "This is creepy. Molly doesn't look anything like . . . Molly."

Jace nodded, feeling uneasy and strange again. Then he felt himself getting angry once more. This would have been fun and interesting if he didn't have to worry about Mr. Hiss. Abram made a little sound and Jace looked back at Ms. Seale. She was holding Molly's hands, urging her to stand up so that everyone could get a good look at her face. Molly giggled. Jace felt almost sick. The effect was awful. Molly's scaly face wrinkled up and she looked like a giggling snake with hair. Jace dug his fingers into the wood of his desk.

"Cool," Brett said very clearly from the back of the room. "Really cool."

"Are you ready to see yourself?" Ms. Seale asked Molly. "It might be a little bit of a shock.

Just remember that all of this will come right off."

Molly nodded. "I want to see." She giggled again and raised her hands.

"No, don't touch it," Ms. Seale said quickly, "or you'll smear everything." Molly's hands hovered for a second, then she let them fall to her sides again. Ms. Seale reached into the box and took out a mirror. "Here you go."

Molly took the mirror and raised it slowly. She took a heavy breath and turned away from the class, then brought the mirror closer and looked into it. She made an odd sound, almost like she was going to cry. Instantly, Ms. Seale touched Molly's shoulders. "Let me take a picture of it so that you can show people that you were an alien. Then we'll take it off." Molly nodded, still staring into the mirror. Ms. Seale turned to Mr. Hiss. "You have the camera?" He nodded and bent to open a drawer.

Ms. Seale took three or four pictures, from different angles. The class was noisy now; everyone was talking about how strange Molly looked. Abram kept shifting nervously around in his seat but he didn't turn around. Jace was grateful. It was bad enough, looking at Molly like this. He knew that he wouldn't relax until she looked normal again.

"It all comes off with cold cream," Ms. Seale reassured Molly. She guided Molly back to her chair and began the process of removing the makeup. Mr. Hiss started writing homework assignments on the board.

"We're out of time, kids, but maybe Ms. Seale can come back sometime. Just copy these down," Mr. Hiss said over his shoulder, "and bring the work in tomorrow."

Startled, Jace looked at the clock. It was almost two-thirty. The dismissal bell would ring in four minutes. How had the afternoon gone by so quickly? He pulled paper out of his notebook and began copying the assignments. He couldn't wait to be out in the sunshine, out in the cold afternoon air. He glanced up at Molly. Her face was almost back to normal. He felt a relief so deep that for a second he was afraid that he might cry.

Mr. Hiss handed Molly a piece of paper. "I wrote the homework down for you." He smiled and winked at Ms. Seale. Molly thanked him and started for her seat just as the bell rang. The class shuffled papers and people began getting up. Brett Kirston was the first one to the door, but he hesitated, waiting for Molly. Abram stood up and Jace met his eyes. Jace wondered if he looked as upset as Abram did.

"I have to take this back to the library," Abram

said apologetically. He held up a book. "It's due today."

Jace nodded. "I'll go with you."

Abram slung his backpack over his shoulder. "Let's get out of here."

Jace nodded in agreement. They went out the door, without looking back. Halfway across the playground, Abram turned to Jace.

"I don't know what to think."

Jace nodded. "I know what you mean. Ms. Seale seemed nice. But Mr. Hiss seems nice. And he's the principal . . ."

Abram slowed his pace a little, looking into Jace's eyes. "I know. Unless we go to the police . . ."

Jace groaned, interrupting him. "And what are we going to tell them? That we think our substitute teacher is a creature from outer space. They'll decide that the makeup demonstration gave our little imaginations too many ideas." He glanced up. "Let's hurry. The last thing I need is to miss the bus."

Abram nodded and shouldered the push-bar on the library door, turning around so that he was still facing Jace. "If we miss it, I'll call my mom. She won't be upset."

Jace followed Abram in, walking to the big window that overlooked the parking lot. He stopped, startled. The little red VW was parked on this side of the lot today. And Mr. Hiss was standing right outside the glass—less than twenty feet away. Ms. Seale was beside him. They were talking. Ms. Seale laughed, tilting her head back. They both faced the windows, and Jace realized that they were looking at themselves in the mirrored surface. Mr. Hiss touched Ms. Seale's face. She reached up to smooth her hair, like a woman standing in front of a mirror.

"Come on," Abram whispered from behind him.

Without saying anything, Jace pointed out the window. He heard Abram take in a sharp breath.

As they stood, looking through the dark glass, Mr. Hiss said something that made Ms. Seale laugh again. Mr. Hiss reached forward and put his fingers around her throat. She stopped laughing and tried to push his hands away. Mr. Hiss shook his head, still talking. Abruptly he pushed his thumbs into her throat and peeled back her skin.

Jace cried out softly, too terrified to move. Ms. Seale's skin wrinkled under the pressure of Mr. Hiss's hands. Her face crumpled and lifted, collapsing as Mr. Hiss pulled harder. Her hair lifted, too, coming away with her scalp. But there was no blood.

For an instant, Ms. Seale stood still, her eyes wide in her snake-blue face. Jace swallowed, trying to understand. Ms. Seale wasn't pretty and blonde anymore. She looked just like Molly had. Her face had the same odd shape, with a raised brow and not quite human cheeks, and the same scaly, bluish skin. Jace squeezed his eyes shut, then opened them.

In the instant that he had looked away, Ms. Seale had gotten into the little VW. She had slouched down in the seat, hiding. Jace was shaking, slowly understanding what he had seen. No wonder Ms. Seale was a makeup artist. She had to make herself look human every day. Mr. Hiss had just pulled off her mask. Jace stared out the window.

Ms. Seale looked like she was laughing again, her alien blue skin hidden by the tinted windshield. From this distance, her face looked only a little odd, slightly misshapen. Jace imagined that he could hear her laughing, in her normal, human-sounding voice. Mr. Hiss was laughing too. Helpless to do anything but watch, Jace stood numbly while Mr. Hiss started his car, then backed up and drove out of the parking lot.

"I feel sick," Abram said.

Jace could only nod.

Saturday morning was bright and sunny again—
and cold. Jace's parents left, reminding him to
take his key and to be careful. "Going bike riding?" his mother asked from the doorway. Jace
nodded.

"I have theater group but we did errands last
night, so we'll be back here in an hour or so. Call
and tell us if you go to Abram's afterward." Jace
nodded again. Then they were gone. When the
door closed Jace ran to get ready.

His mother's camera was in the hall closet. He
picked dark pants and a drab green shirt. He was
waiting in the driveway when Abram pedalled
up.

Jace could see his own breath as they rode up
Brace Street. Abram was a little ways behind and
Jace slowed to let him catch up. They turned onto
Garland together. The Garland Street hill seemed

too steep, and too short. Suddenly, Jace was at the end of the street, leaning into a wide, uneasy circle. Abram followed him around and they circled three or four times, glancing at each other. Finally, Jace braked and reluctantly swung his leg over.

Abram stopped and sat astride on his bike. He pushed up his glasses. "I tried to call the police last night," he said in a hoarse, low voice. "The officer just laughed at me. Then he hung up."

"Abram, no one is going to believe us." Jace leaned back against his bike, his eyes darting nervously up the curving driveway.

Abram scuffed his shoe on the pavement. "It's like a movie, you know that? If they think we're serious, they're going to make counselor's appointments. If they think we're kidding, they'll ignore us completely, or punish us for making things up. We have to be able to prove it."

Jace sighed. They had been talking about this all week, and they just kept saying the same things, over and over. He patted the little bike pack that held his mother's camera. "That's why we're here, right?" He looked up the drive again. "We should hide. What if he drives out right now?"

Abram frowned, pushing his glasses up. "Okay. Okay."

Jace felt a surge of anger. "You can go home if you don't want to do this."

Abram looked startled. "I didn't say that."

Jace mumbled an apology. "I'm just scared, that's all." He unzipped the pack and took out the camera. Then he glanced back up.

Abram was nodding. "Me, too. Maybe we shouldn't."

Jace shook his head fiercely, the flash of anger coming back, warming him, raising his courage. "I'm going up there." He pointed, stabbing a finger toward the old Victorian house. "I'm going to find out what's going on once and for all." Abruptly he began walking, shoving his bike along, going fifty feet or so up the driveway before he stopped. He was so nervous that his stomach hurt, and his hands were so sweaty that he was afraid he would drop the camera. He lifted the strap and hung it around his neck. Then he pushed his bike forward into the bushes.

Once his bike was concealed, Jace looked back. Abram looked jittery as he hid his bike. But he turned and nodded once he had it far enough back in the bushes. "I'm ready."

"Let's go?" Jace didn't mean for it to sound like a question, but at least his voice didn't sound as shaky as he felt. Abram nodded slowly and together they started up the little road.

100

Once they could see the house, Jace held up one hand and squatted behind a bush that jutted out into the driveway. Abram came up beside him, duck-walking in order to stay low.

"See anything?"

Jace shook his head, scanning the porch and the raked flower beds. He could see a little patch of bright red toward the rear of the house that told him the little VW was there. But he couldn't see anything else. The big front window caught the morning sun and flashed it back toward them like a mirror. "The car is there. So he's home."

Abram half-stood, peering through the tangle of grayish twigs. "Let's go closer."

Jace swallowed hard, but he nodded. If they were ever going to be able to prove anything about Mr. Hiss, they would have to take chances.

Slowly, they advanced toward the house. After a few steps, they fell into single file, with Jace leading the way. He went slowly, hesitating, his eyes moving constantly over the porch, the road, the little side yard where the VW was parked—then back again. He turned to whisper. "I wish we could see inside."

Abram murmured an assent. Jace turned to check the road behind them.

Suddenly Abram grabbed Jace's shoulder. "Quick. Hide. They're coming." Jace nearly lost his balance as he straightened and leapt into the bushes. He heard his jacket tear as it caught on a twig, but he ignored it. Abram was beside him, working his way into the bushes just a few feet away.

Jace turned back toward the house and crouched. He could hear Abram's clothes snagging on the bushes, then there was only the sound of Abram's ragged breath, and his own thudding heart.

Seconds passed. Jace's eyes were watering and he rubbed his sleeve across his face. He squinted up at the sky. The sun was still pale and winter-cold. Just then Abram made a tiny clicking sound with his tongue. "Can you see them?" Jace jerked his head around, struggling to see through the crisscrossing maze of twigs. He drew in a long breath. Mr. Hiss and Ms. Seale were on the porch of the house.

Mr. Hiss was standing with his hands on his hips. Ms. Seale was pacing back and forth, turning abruptly to face him when she reached the end of the porch. Her heavy blonde hair swung when she turned. She looked normal again. You would never have known that she was an alien. Or whatever she was. Jace shook his head, watching Mr. Hiss stare out at the trees that surrounded the front yard. After a moment, Mr. Hiss shook his head and turned back toward Ms. Seale.

They were talking now. Jace could hear their voices, but it was difficult to make out what they were saying. They faced each other and kept talking, their voices too soft to make out. Then, as Jace watched, Mr. Hiss raised both hands and shook his head. He walked quickly toward Ms. Seale, gesturing.

"No. No. It has to be more sudden." The words were clear, even though Mr. Hiss was facing away from them now. He was almost shouting. Ms. Seale shook her head. She was frowning, and she said something that Jace couldn't hear well enough to understand, but she looked upset. Jace leaned forward, wishing he could hear better. Mr. Hiss gestured again, walking away. "Halfway then. From the screams." He was speaking loudly again, and the words were very clear. Jace glanced at Abram. Nothing made sense. What were they talking about? Why would two aliens be standing on a porch as if they were two normal people? Or why would two normal people be talking nonsense? Jace shivered, remembering how Ms. Seale's human face had peeled away, leaving her alien face exposed. Did Mr. Hiss wear the same kind of makeup every day? Jace swallowed. Probably. That was why he looked so

103

weird. Jace looked back over his shoulder at Abram.

Even through the tangle of twigs he could see that Abram's face was intent and pale as he stared toward the porch. Jace watched him. He wanted their lives to be as simple as they had been before they'd met Mr. Hiss. Jace looked back toward the porch just as Ms. Seale whirled and screamed. Jace clenched his jaw. He heard Abram take in a quick, startled breath.

Ms. Seale screamed again. It was an awful scream, terrible. Mr. Hiss hurried toward her, saying something in a low, threatening tone of voice. Jace heard Abram gasp again as Mr. Hiss took Ms. Seale by her shoulders and began to shake her. Her hair swung wildly along the sides of her face. Then, without warning, she reached up and ripped at her own throat. Hands clawing frantically, she lifted her human makeup—just as Mr. Hiss had done in the parking lot. Mr. Hiss stumbled backward, crying out in obvious terror. Jace frowned. They had both laughed before. Why was Mr. Hiss so scared of her now?

"It doesn't make sense," Abram whispered, echoing his thought. Jace nodded. It seemed like a long time since anything had made sense. He raised the camera, but his hands were shaking so hard that he knew that he would never manage to take a picture.

Suddenly, Ms. Seale made an odd, gurgling sound. She raised one arm, pointing at Mr. Hiss, as though her hand were a weapon. He staggered backward, crying out a second time. He stumbled and almost fell as she came toward him. Jace felt a sheen of sweat break out on his forehead. They had seemed like friends. What was happening? Was she going to hurt him? Mr. Hiss scrabbled backward, flinching and cowering. Ms. Seale continued to stalk him, moving closer and closer.

"No," Mr. Hiss screamed. Ms. Seale raised her arm again, elbow straight, her eyes slitted almost shut in her weird blue-scaled face. She made the strange gurgling, choking noise again. Mr. Hiss toppled over as though something had hit him. He jerked, his whole body twitching. Ms. Seale threw back her head and laughed. It was a high pulsing sound, not like a human laugh at all.

Jace watched helplessly as she took one step toward Mr. Hiss, then another. Maybe Mr. Hiss wasn't an alien, Jace thought suddenly. Maybe Ms. Seale was making him do things. Maybe they weren't friends at all, and she was about to really hurt him. Ms. Seale extended her arm again. Mr. Hiss gasped out a last cry and collapsed. Jace could see a red stain spreading across his shirt.

Blood? But she hadn't touched him and Jace couldn't see anything in her hand. Ms. Seale raised her arm again.

"Get away from him," Jace yelled without thinking. His voice was raspy and painful, but he kept yelling. "Leave him alone. Get away from him!"

"Jace," Abram hissed, wrenching at his arm, pulling him down. Jace covered his mouth with his hand, astonished. He hadn't meant to yell. He shook his head, confused, then looked back at the porch. Ms. Seale had come down the steps and she was walking toward them! Behind her, Mr. Hiss was struggling to his feet. Ms. Seale turned and called out to him, but Jace couldn't understand what she said. Her eyes were still narrow, squinting out of her bluish face. She spun around, Jace caught a weird reddish tint from her eyes. She raised her arm to point at them.

"Run!" Jace shrieked. Abram leapt up and lunged his way out of the bushes. Jace was right behind him, the twigs raking at his face and hands until he burst onto the road and started running.

"Wait," Ms. Seale yelled at them. "Wait." Her voice sounded too high, alien, and Jace felt an ache of fear go through his legs. Still, he ran faster, pounding along just behind Abram. As they ran, the sound of Ms. Seale's voice weakened.

Jace dragged in long breaths and ran faster. She wasn't following them. Or if she was, aliens couldn't run very fast. Abram was still ahead of him when they got to the end of the drive. Jace hesitated, almost stumbling. Maybe they should just run and not get their bikes at all. But Abram was already slowing, sliding to a stop, looking frantically at the wall of gray-brown twigs. Jace stumbled to a stop beside him, breathing so hard that it almost hurt. He shot a glance back up the driveway but they had rounded the curve and he couldn't see Ms. Seale, or Mr. Hiss. He couldn't even see the house.

"Where did we . . ." Abram whirled to face him and Jace shook his head, helplessly scanning the bushes. He couldn't see even the tiniest flash of color, couldn't remember just how far into the driveway they had come before they'd hidden their bikes. He looked up the driveway again. This time, what he saw made his stomach churn.

Mr. Hiss and Ms. Seale were running toward them, yelling and gesturing.

"There," Abram screamed. He dragged Jace around and pointed into the bushes. Then he lunged forward. Jace could see the light green curve of his bike fender. Shaking, he glanced once more up the road. Mr. Hiss and Ms. Seale had slowed a little, but they were still coming toward them. The red stain on Mr. Hiss's shirt had widened. Jace plunged into the bushes. Seconds later he was swinging one leg over his bike, trying to control the trembling in his knees so that he could pedal. A few seconds after that, he was following Abram back out onto Garland Street, sucking clean air into his lungs, hearing the shouts behind them grow softer and farther away.

All the way up the long Garland Street hill, Jace kept twisting to look back over his shoulder.

"Stop looking, you're going to ride right into me," Abram shouted near the top.

Jace nodded. "Sorry. I'm just . . ." He paused, trying to catch his breath. "I'm just . . ."

"Scared," Abram finished for him. "Me, too. What are they doing? I thought she'd killed him."

Jace shook his head. "I don't know. We have to call . . ." he paused to drag in one breath, then another, "we have to call the police."

Abram nodded as they topped the hill. "From your house. It's closer."

Jace made himself stand up on the pedals, and forced his screaming muscles to shut up and work. Abram stayed right beside him as they rounded the corner and headed down Brace Street. They were almost all the way to Porter when Jace saw Abram turn to look behind them. "Oh, no. Jace, hurry!"

Jace looked over his shoulder. The little red VW was rounding the Brace Street corner. At this distance, it would be hard for them to recognize him and Abram. But in less than a minute, they would be close enough to do more than that.

"We can make it onto Porter before they're sure it's us," he shouted to Abram. "Hurry." Jace pumped harder than he ever had in his life. Abram dropped back a little, but not much. Jace faced forward, pedalling with his whole concentration. He kept imagining the sewing-machine rhythm of the VW engine coming closer, closer. As they turned right onto Porter, he risked one quick glance and fought an impulse to cry out.

He hadn't been imagining anything. Mr. Hiss and Ms. Seale were right behind them—and the minute he turned to look, he saw Mr. Hiss nod briskly at Ms. Seale. She leaned out the window, her blue-skinned alien's face contorted.

"Kids. Hey, kids!"

Using what felt like the last of his strength, Jace shoved at his bike pedals.

"Hey, kids. Please!"

Ms. Seale's voice was closer, or maybe she was just yelling louder. Jace refused to look. He kept his eyes on his house, less than a half a block away now. "We're almost there," he gasped and he saw Abram nod. Then he noticed the empty driveway. "My parents aren't back yet." Jace glanced at Abram and saw him nod again, his face contorted like he was about to start crying.

Together they turned into the yard, braking and sliding. Jace dropped his bike and stumbled once, jumping over it to race for the front door. Jamming his hand into his pocket as he went, he fished for his key. The camera bounced painfully against his chest, startling him. He had forgotten it was there.

"Hey, please! Kids!"

Ms. Seale was still yelling as Jace jabbed the key into the lock and wrenched it around, flinging the door open. "Lock it behind us," he shouted at Abram, and hesitated just long enough to watch Abram make it inside and whirl to slam the door. Then he ran for the phone.

Breathing in gasps, Jace grabbed the receiver. His hands felt huge, clumsy, and he dropped it twice before he managed to punch at the buttons with shaking fingers.

"Emergency Line. How can I help?"

"There's an alien," Jace began, then stopped. He would have to start at the beginning. He took a huge breath and started over. "Our substitute teacher, his name is Mr. Hiss and he seemed really weird so we followed him and he lives in this old abandoned house and . . ."

"Please speak more slowly."

Jace tried to steady his voice. "I . . . we saw a murder, but he isn't dead," Jace stuttered. "And she's an alien."

He heard the operator exhale sharply.

"The one who killed our teacher, I mean," Jace added desperately. "Just listen, please."

The operator clicked her tongue. "I am listening. Please try to calm down a little."

Jace tried to swallow and couldn't. "I—see— the first thing was that he had blood all over his face. Then there were his eyes . . ."

"Is someone there with you?"

Jace swallowed and tried to calm his breathing. "Only Abram. Our substitute teacher got . . . I mean he's an alien, maybe. But she is, I know that for sure and they are trying to get in."

"Young man, this is not a good place for jokes," the operator scolded him. "This line is for people who really need help."

A second later the line went dead in Jace's ear. He lowered the receiver and stared at it, unable to think. A loud knocking at the front door broke his numbness. He ran back up the hall into the living room. Abram was standing flat-footed, staring at the front door with his fists clenched.

A tapping sound at the window made him jerk around. Abram groaned again. There, at the window, was Ms. Seale. She was gesturing frantically, pointing and talking. Her alien blue lips were forming words that Jace couldn't hear.

Jace shook his head and grabbed Abram's arm. "We have to get out of here." He glanced back at the window. Ms. Seale was still waving and motioning at them, but he saw something else. Something worse, in a way. His parents were pulling up. He watched his mother park the car, saw her lean to say something to his father as she bent to set the emergency brake. Then she got out, her face stern and worried, and walked straight toward Ms. Seale. Ms. Seale turned and saw her coming. And then she raised her arm.

Panicked, Jace shoved past Abram and flung the door open. Mr. Hiss was standing on the porch. Jace shoved past him. "Mom! Don't come any closer. Get back in the car. Dad! Dad! Go now, run!"

Jace's mother looked from Ms. Seale's blue, alien face, to Mr. Hiss, then back again. She smiled. "I think we can straighten all this out in a few minutes. But Jace is going to be pretty upset. I would be." She turned and looked at Jace's father. He nodded.

Jace felt the grip of his father's warm hand on

his shoulder as he went past. "Calm down, Jace. It really is all right."

Jace felt his mouth drop open, and he couldn't close it. "What are you talking . . . ?" he managed.

His mother nodded again, this time at Ms. Seale and Mr. Hiss. "Come in, please."

Jace's knees felt stiff and wooden as his father guided him and Abram into the living room. He watched helplessly as Ms. Seale and Mr. Hiss sat side by side on the couch. He and Abram stayed on their feet, too nervous to sit down.

"You know this is just makeup," Ms. Seale said when she saw him staring at her face. "I did it in class. The same face, exactly."

Jace nodded. "But . . . your other face?"

Ms. Seale smiled and reached up to touch her scaled face. "See?" She scraped her fingers over her cheek. The scales smeared and the plastic shape beneath came up in her hand. Jace stared, bewildered.

"I had on a mask over this that day at school," Ms. Seale explained. "A latex mask made from my own face. We wanted to see if anyone could tell. It's all part of a movie Jack and I are involved in. So was the blood and the screaming, and all the rest. I am so sorry that you were frightened."

114

Jace looked at his mother. "So I didn't imagine anything."

His mother sighed. "I thought you had. I admit it. Then this morning I saw this down at the Community Theater." She opened her purse and took out a bright yellow piece of paper. She handed it to Jace.

NOW HIRING ACTORS AND EXTRAS the heading on the paper said. Then there were two columns of print below. "Local student filmmakers are now preparing to begin an ambitious science fiction film," the paper explained. "Pay will be low, but involvement in the project should be fun and interesting. Much will be learned about full-face makeup and other special effects including use of fake eyeballs, blood, and 'alien' red contact lenses, forced perspective camera work and many other fanciful and horrifying techniques of film."

"Look here," his mother interrupted him. She stood up to point. Jace focused on the words. It was a single line, at the very bottom of the page. "Please contact Mr. Jack Hiss." And there was a phone number.

For the first time, Mr. Hiss spoke. "What you saw was a rehearsal. Ms. Seale and I were practicing a scene for the film."

"What about the eyeballs?" Abram demanded

115

from the kitchen doorway. Jace turned to look at him, then back at Mr. Hiss.

Mr. Hiss's eyes widened in surprise. "The eyeballs?"

"The ones in the bowl on your porch. You licked your finger . . ." Abram said angrily and then he blushed. "We were just trying to figure things out and we spied on you. I'm sorry . . ."

Mr. Hiss raised his hand. "Don't apologize. It's all for the film, too. We make the blood out of syrup, red coloring, flour, and tiny amounts of black ink. It's sticky, and sweet. I know it must have looked awful if I did that, but . . . it's just syrup, really." He stopped and ran his hands through his hair, looking down at his red-stained chest. "If there ever is something dangerous in this town, I hope you two are on my side. Darlene—Ms. Seale and I were talking about it on the way here. If I thought what you two thought, I would never have had the courage that you two showed."

Jace's father was nodding. He looked proud. Jace felt one of the biggest knots in his stomach begin to loosen. "And the blood in that little room off the library?"

Mr. Hiss groaned. "I thought the door opened. I washed up quickly and went out . . . I remember now. You two were there. Poor Jace. And then there was the day when I had the red contacts in. I hoped you hadn't noticed, or I would have said something. But I've kept an eye on you and you seemed so normal and attentive in class . . . well." He ran his hands though his hair again. "I owe you an apology. Both of you." He nodded at Abram.

Jace stared at Mr. Hiss without saying anything. Then he looked at Abram. "It's okay. I guess." Abram nodded.

Mr. Hiss smiled. "Thank you. I'll make it up to you if you'll let me. Would you like to help with the movie?"

Jace glanced at his mother's attentive expression and managed a smile. "She would."

Mr. Hiss looked at his mother and she grinned. "I do a little acting. The local theater group, a few small movie parts. It's a hobby."

Mr. Hiss nodded. "We have lots of parts. Come to the casting call, and we'll find something you'll have fun at."

"She's good," Jace interrupted. "Really good."

Mr. Hiss laughed. "Maybe one of the bigger parts, then. And how about you two?"

Abram and Jace exchanged another glance. "Be in the movie?" Abram asked.

"Absolutely," Ms. Seale said without hesitating. "You've earned it."

Jace shook his head. Brett was going to be jealous. So would half the kids in the school. Even if he never liked watching scary movies, it might be fun to be in one. He nodded and looked at Abram.

"Sure," Abram said finally. "Sure. That'd be great."

Ms. Seale stood up. Her smeared makeup looked weird. "We should be going. I need to wash up."

Mr. Hiss got up, too. He looked straight at Jace. "I never meant to upset you two. I really am sorry."

Jace smiled at him. "I'm just glad that nothing awful is happening. I thought . . ." He shook his head. "How did you just point and . . ." He looked at Mr. Hiss's stained shirt, then at Ms. Seale. She laughed.

"We'll show you. You'll like the costumes too. There's a lot of makeup involved, and one of the characters is a huge furry creature that—"

"In your trunk," Jace interrupted her, looking at Mr. Hiss.

Mr. Hiss smiled and shook his head. "You don't miss anything. I took the fur costume to the cleaners one day."

Jace felt his stomach settling again, the knots unraveling, his muscles relaxing in a way that they hadn't in a long time. Mr. Hiss stood and

118

extended his hand. Jace came forward to shake it. He let out a big breath. Monday morning he would wake up and feel good about going to school again. He looked up to see Abram grinning at him.

It was over.

It was finally over.

I knew there was no turning back now. This was it.

I took a deep breath, stomped the thick black mud off my boots, and opened the front door to the Cape Flattery Veterinary Clinic.

I stood for a minute just inside the entrance, dripping puddles onto the linoleum floor and remembering another stormy Christmas Eve three years ago, right after we moved to Cape Flattery, when Mom gave me Howard as a puppy. It was our first Christmas without Dad.

"Dr. Holmes?" I tried to keep my voice steady.

"I'm in the operating room, Billy."

I followed the voice down the dimly-lit hallway and found the operating room at the end.

Inside, Dr. Holmes was standing beside a large metal table. Howard was lying on top of it, held down by long leather straps. "I waited for you, Billy, but I was hoping you wouldn't come. I don't really think it's a good idea for you to be here when I put Howard to sleep."

"I have to. I promised Howard I'd stay with him."

Dr. Holmes shrugged. "Well, let's get it over with then."

I watched as Dr. Holmes took a long needle and filled it with a clear liquid.

All of a sudden everything seemed to be happening in slow motion, but I knew it was probably because my mind was wanting to slow down Howard's death.

"It'll be painless, Billy. This is a new drug. Howard'll think he's back home, ready to take a nice, long nap."

How does he know that? I wondered.

"I'm really sorry, Billy, but it's either this or a lawsuit against your mother," Dr. Holmes continued, "and you know she couldn't afford that."

"Please hurry." I knew Dr. Holmes was only trying to make me feel better about the whole thing, but I wasn't quite sure how much longer I could stand to be there.

Dr. Holmes aimed the long needle at Howard's stomach.

My head throbbed and my heart pounded.

"The needle's in," Dr. Holmes said quietly. "I'm injecting the solution now."

I locked eyes with the dark brown pools that belonged to my dog. I wasn't quite sure whether I was seeing disbelief or betrayal, or if dogs even knew about those things.

Slowly, the brown pools began to lose their depth, and I knew the end was near, but I couldn't take my eyes away from Howard's.

Then his eyelids lowered.

I felt like crying out, but I promised myself I wouldn't.

Howard's eyelids continued slowly downward.

"It won't be long now," Dr. Holmes whispered.

Above us, the fluorescent lights suddenly flickered.

Dr. Holmes looked up. "I hope they don't go out. We'll be in the dark for sure, without any windows in here."

A loud crash of thunder shook the room.

"What the . . ." Dr. Holmes said.

The flickering lights had now become strobes, and everything in the room seemed out of focus.

Another crash of thunder forced me to grab hold of the operating table.

"I hate these winter storms," Dr. Holmes muttered.

Then the flickering stopped. The lights seemed to grow brighter.

Howard's eyes opened wide, and the brown pools were deeper than I had ever seen them before.

They drew me into them. I could hardly breathe. I felt as if I was drowning. I held on to the side of the metal operating table even tighter.

The lights began to flicker again, this time even more wildly, and thunder literally caused the room to tremble.

Then Howard closed his eyes completely, and the lights went out.

I held my breath.

"What was that all about?" Dr. Holmes finally said.

"He'll be back," I whispered. "Howard's coming back from the dead!"